SCHOOL'S

SUCH A

BUMMER!

MARNI DUGGAN

THIS IS FOR GROOVY FREEDOMS
EVERYWHERE.

THIS BOOK IS A WORK OF FICTION.
INCIDENTS, NAMES, CHARACTERS
AND PLACES ARE PRODUCTS OF THE
AUTHOR'S IMAGINATION AND USED
FICTITIOUSLY. RESEMBLANCES TO
ACTUAL INCIDENTS, NAMES,
CHARACTERS AND PLACES
ARE STRICTLY COINCIDENTAL.

1

I HAD JUST gotten into my teens the first time I saw a police officer for real. He pulled me over and asked to see my driver's license. I said, "I don't have one. I'm only thirteen." He told me I was under arrest, and I wasn't sure what that was all about, either.

But then they started putting Weed into the ambulance, so I didn't care much about the arrest, even the handcuffs.

"Where's the pink slip for this truck?" the cop asked.

I had no idea what a pink slip was. I always thought pink was a beautiful color, so maybe she would get one for the truck.

"The pink slip," he repeated. "The ownership paper. Who owns this truck?"

"It belongs to everyone." That's what Weed had always said. "Nobody owns anything, yet everybody owns everything."

"Where do you live?" he asked.

"Rosemead Farm."

"Oh, *that* place."

I grinned. The cops, and everyone else, stayed out of Rosemead because they didn't understand us.

That's what Weed loved so much about our home. He had no use for money, the stuff it would buy and all the people who craved money for its buying power.

"Hippies," the cop muttered, as if it were the worst kind of dirty word.

I nodded. "Weed was a hippie years ago. Rosemead? It had dozens of families at one point. Now it's just Weed and me." I looked towards the nursing station. "I sure hope he's feeling better now."

The police officer sneered. "Who is 'Weed'? His identification says he's Lawrence Jay Levenson."

"He answers to Weed, and he's my uncle." I added, "He's hurt because he fell off a ladder."

"Why was a man his age on a ladder?"

"Painting the house," I said. "He lost his balance. Usually he has good balance."

"So you got into the truck and drove him to get help."

I shrugged. "Yep. I drive all the time. Weed taught me to drive as soon as I was tall enough. He taught me to read when I was three."

The police wiped some sweat from his forehead. "When your grandfather fell, why didn't you just dial nine-one-one?"

"We don't have a phone," I replied. "We've never had one. Weed says we don't need one. We can use the one they have in the nearest town."

He looked me up and down for the longest time, as if trying to decide if I was putting him on. Finally, he asked, "What's your name, young lady?"

"Groovy. Groovy Freedom."

He nodded and took off the handcuffs.

Why would a teenager like me allow my old uncle get on a ladder and paint our house? Well, why not?

Weed taught me practically everything I knew. He homeschooled me, and I loved every moment of it. The law said I had to get an education *somewhere, somehow,* and they tested me every year to see the results of my daily sessions with Weed. I don't think any school bus would have made it all the way to Rosemead in that rugged part of the world. Also, Weed would have nixed the idea of sending me to a public or private school. "They're all mills," he'd said. "They teach you *not* to think. They just want you to do your slave work, pay your bills and keep your mouth shut."

So I was studying when Weed fell. I had a question or two about that day's lesson, so I went outside and said, "Weed…"

He took his eyes off his work and adjusted his feet. He lost his footing and down he went.

"Ouch!"

"Weed—" At first, I thought he was dead.

He looked up at me and smiled, as if to make me think he was OK, which he wasn't. "Groovy—"

I got to my feet. "I'll get Doc Dawson."

He grabbed my arm and shook his head. "Dawson's a vet. This time we need an M.D."

"Dawson's taken care of us pretty well so far," I told him.

"Just get me into the truck and take me to the hospital. I've really banged myself up this time."

Weed maintains that anger makes a person ill. The

anger feeds on itself, so the angrier a person becomes, the sicker he feels. You're also harming yourself more than the person you're getting mad at.

Slipping and falling off the ladder must have made him forget that particular bit of wisdom, because when the nurses let me in to see him, he was yelling, and I *do* mean yelling, at the doctor. *"I can't do physiotherapy! I have a farm and a kid to look after! Let me out of here!"*

"You can't go home. You have injuries. You need to have an operation." The doctor spoke in a calm voice. I got the impression that throughout his medical career he had told many patients things they did not want to hear and they had sassed him plenty. He probably just let it go in one ear and out the other.

"Which part of 'let me out of here' did you fail to understand?" Weed was now too tired to yell. "I have a niece. I need to look after her."

"Why is she *your* responsibility?" the doctor wanted to know. "What about her parents?"

"Dead and gone. They went to Africa to teach the men to wear condoms."

The truth is much, much less tragic. My parents had me, then they took off for Africa because they wanted to be there instead of here. They left me with Weed, and I saw my folks only in a handful of pictures. Back then in Rosemead, everyone sort of belonged to everyone else, so it became hard to figure out who was related to whom. Throughout it all, Weed never let me forget that I was the most-loved little girl who ever lived, and I was certainly the happiest kid I knew.

At my uncle's beside, I stood over him and held his hand.

8

He looked up at me and frowned. "We have a bummer, Groovy. And what do we say when we have a bummer?"

I nodded. "We can work it out, we can work it out," I sang. We had handled bummers in that way for a very long time. Even though Rosemead was just him and me now, he always consulted me on decisions that had to be made, and he treated me like an intelligent human being with feelings.

The doctor scratched his head and said, "This child must have someone out there who could take her in. A family friend or someone from school...?"

"I teach her," said Weed.

"Look, Mister Levenson—"

"Folks call me Weed. You can, too."

"OK, Mister Weed—"

"No, not 'Mister Weed.' Just Weed."

The doctor rolled his eyes. "Weed, we'll have to do surgery on you tomorrow. I'll call the social worker to see about arrangements for the girl."

That was the moment when I knew Weed and I wouldn't be allowed to work out our bummer by ourselves.

2

From the mind of…
MRS. DAVIS

I WALKED INTO that room, saw her standing there in her bellbottoms, headband and granny glasses, and I said to myself, *Rosemead Farm lives on.* Nobody had worn that kind of clothing since the very early '70s, and nobody wore it today except at costume parties. Even in the Haight-Ashbury, the neighborhood where everyone was a hippie in 1967, they dressed today like normal people.

She seemed full of anxiety, and I felt for her. I knew how difficult the adjustment would be for her once she entered public school.

"Hi," I said. "I'm Mrs. Davis."

She smiled the way a child would if a stranger came up and offered her candy. "I'm Groovy."

Wasn't that just some kind of name? My own name, Chris, was short for Christmas.

I had moved out of Rosemead a few decades earlier, but the sight of Groovy made me flash back on psychedelic colors, bead-stringing, be-ins and the Summer of Love.

I was barely old enough for school when my folks decided to drop out of society and drop into Rosemead. I can't remember life before that commune. For a half-dozen years all I knew was Rosemead. I wore colorful, funky, handmade dresses, didn't know what shoes were, watched my mom and dad sort of swap partners with the other moms and dads, pretended to know what the Vietnam War was, helped around the farm and listened to way too much Bob Dylan and Joan Baez music.

It all seemed normal enough to me until my parents decided that being a hippie was just too hard. So we went back to the "squares." I remember that time much too clearly—little Christmas the hippie waif, who slept outdoors when she felt like it and smiled at everyone she met, taken away and put into a new world where everybody almost hated and feared each other.

I smiled at Groovy Freedom and myself when I was her age. She had spent her young life living in a time that no longer existed. The only thing about the Sixties that people liked today was the music.

I had the name of a foster family that was willing to take her in, but I decided against it.

"Groovy," I told her, "I think I'm going to take you home with me for a little while."

"What a drag," she said. "I have to get back to the farm and start picking fruit. Everything's getting ripe. I need to get it together before Weed gets home."

I remembered Weed from way back when. He was one of the first hippies at Rosemead, maybe even the first. He was sort of the boss there, if it was possible for hippies to *have* a boss. He was tall and strong, with a loud voice. I tried to stay away from him.

"Hold on for a second." I paused and thought. "Is Lawrence Jay Levenson also known as Weed?"

Groovy beamed at me. "Right on! Have you met him?"

"I used to live at the farm. Years and years ago.

I'm sure Weed would want you to stay with someone who knows about Rosemead."

Groovy nodded, not looking too thrilled to be going home with me.

3

I HAD NOTHING but friends and admirers as I sauntered down the aisle of the school bus. They offered me their palms to slap, they blew me kisses and winked at me.

"You go, girl!"

"Wassup, girlfriend?"

"It's all good," I told them…and it was. In fact, it was *awesome!*

Once I got off the bus, I looked up and smiled at the lovely September day, the beginning of what I knew would be one of the most wonderful years of my life. As head cheerleader and member of every club worth joining, I was our school's Big Woman on Campus. After two years of being an "underclassman," I was at the top. Yea!

Each morning, I woke up and said out loud, "Being me is lots of fun."

Well, maybe there was one little problem. I looked up and saw the problem. The sign said:

WELCOME TO FRANCIS MINUT MIDDLE SCHOOL

The school had gotten the sign fixed. Our boys months ago altered it to say:

WELCOME TO F MINUS MIDDLE SCHOOL

So the sign was back to normal. Bad deal. The boys could always alter the sign again. I would start bugging them about it until they did the alterations.

This year, if I said, "Jump!" people would say, "How high, Heather?" Not that I lacked respect and admiration last year. Last year, I was the most righteous Grade 7 student at F Minus. But you aren't *really* the boss until you're a senior. So now I *was* a senior, and good for me.

I would soon have a good time with the election for Grade 8 president. I didn't want the job for myself. No way! What we did at F Minus was elect the most incompetent student as president. That kid is elected because he or she is the goofiest, dorkiest, most clueless person in the school, a student without any social or administrative skills. So, for the rest of the year, the rest of us get to laugh and point at President Misfit as he or she stumbles through making speeches, running assemblies and doing a dozen other things that he really can't handle.

It can be more fun than an Eddie Murphy movie—if we elect the right doofus.

I thought I had already chosen the right—or wrong—person for the job: Eugene Horowitz. I liked to call him Horror Wits. I had known him since we were about five years old, and over the years I had seen him slapped, tripped, shoved and threatened so many times that I wondered why he hadn't gotten fed up with the abuse and gone for Home Study Option, where the student shows up once a month for ten minutes to get his books and handouts, then does his schoolwork at home.

I walked the hallways of F Minus completely convinced that Horror Wits would be our prez this year. But then something happened.

I was on my way to homeroom, minding my own business, when Mr. Epperman, our principal, got my attention and said, "Heather, I want you to meet a new student." Standing next to him was this creature with long messy blonde hair. She wore a peace-sign headband, a tie-dye T-shirt and the silliest lime-green pants I had ever seen. She was tall and slim, with a bust starting to happen. She might have been pretty if she hadn't tried so hard to look so ugly.

"Heather Marcus, meet Groovy Freedom. Groovy has just transferred here."

I wanted to retort, "Groovy, Planet Fringus just called. They want you home by dinnertime."

"Heather," Epperman said, "show Groovy where locker six-nine-one is and take her to homeroom, OK?"

What really bugged me about Groovy Freedom was that *she* was looking at *me* as if I were some kind of two-headed beast from the pages of *National Geographic*. Hadn't she ever seen a 13-year-old cutie before?

"Come with me, Groovy," I said. "I'll show you where to go."

We walked down the hallway together. People looked at Groovy as if she were a two-headed beast, and they looked at me like, *Heather, where did you get that two-headed beast? And why have you brought it to school?*

"OK," I said. "You've got six-nine-one. Combination is on your registration card. Got it?"

She frowned, shrugged, shook her head. "No."

"Let me see your reg card," I said, plucking it out of her hand. "Combo's right here. Locks are built in, so you don't have to buy your own lock. Don't ever tell anyone your combo, because this place is full of thieves, liars and other nasty people." I said the numbers aloud as I spun the wheel. "Sixteen, twenty-four, forty-five. All done." I opened the locker and said, "It's not very big, but it'll do."

Groovy looked inside. "Dark and empty. What's it for?"

"To put your books and things when you're not using them. So other people can't use them."

"Why do that?"

I frowned. "Why do what?"

"Lock your things away so others can't use them. Wouldn't it be better to make your things available to others, and for others to do the same for you?"

I rolled my eyes. "You should tell that to the school cop. Half his job around here is investigating thefts." Then, "Where did you go to school before you came here?"

"I studied at home. My uncle taught me. Then he fell off a ladder and hurt himself. So here I am."

"So here you are," I replied. Thinking, *Horror Wits, you're off the hook this year.* All of the misfits and outcasts would have an easier time this year because we had a new kid to pick on, and her name was Groovy Freedom. I immediately made a mental note to start grooming her for Grade 8 president.

4

From the mind of...
GROOVY FREEDOM

"HEY, DIPSTICK! QUIT eyeballin' me or I'll pound you!"

"Quit eyeballin' *me*, pizza-face!"

The first kid threw his knapsack into the face of the other kid, who retaliated by punching the first kid in the mouth. Right away they started throwing kicks and punches at each other on the grass near the school's main entrance. They both bled and spat and called each other names that made the other kids laugh or shriek. One boy, punched in the stomach, went down; the other one kicked him until the one on the ground caught the other boy's foot and pulled him down, too.

I watched them, hoping they would stop. I had never seen a fistfight, had never witnessed two human beings unable to resolve their issues through talk, a cup of tea and a handshake. I could smell the boys' dirt and sweat; I could sense their fear and rage. I could hear the *crack!* of fists and feet against faces, and I could not remember ever feeling so afraid of anything or anyone. I wished that Weed was there, to tell me what, if anything, this awful violence meant.

A crowd gathered around the fighters, cheering them on. "Yeah! Do it! Hit him again!"

"Enough!" A tall, muscular man appeared in a gray sweatsuit, waving his arms. "No more! Break it up!" He reached in and pulled apart the fighters, who were much smaller than he was. "All right, who started this thing?"

"*He* started it!" Dipstick and pizza-face yelled, pointing at each other.

The big man turned to the rest of us. "Can anyone here tell me what happened? I want to know who started this fight."

I spoke up. "It started when 'dipstick' hit 'pizza-face' with his knapsack. Then the two of them started punching and kicking each other. It was mostly about 'eyeballing.' That was the main issue."

The big man pointed at me. "Looks like we got Ellen Degeneres here at school today."

"No, that's not my name," I told him. "I'm Groovy Freedom, and this is my first day here."

"You givin' me backtalk, girl?"

"Yessir. Doing my best."

The two fighters smirked at each other. Then they smirked at me. I didn't smirk back.

The big man had some more things to say to me about backtalk and something he called "attitude." Dipstick and pizza-face took off for home and *I* ended up in the principal's office.

I sat in the plastic seat in the office, wondering what I had said or done to get the big man so upset. Then Mrs. Davis entered and said, "Me again."

"Far out!" I beamed. "Is Weed feeling better?"

"Let's hope so. I've come by to get you so that we can go to the hospital and check things out." Then, "Why are you sitting there? That seat is usually for, well…other people."

"The big man said I was full of backtalk and attitude," I told her.

As we were walking down the hallway, Mrs. Davis said, "We have quite a little trip ahead of us. I'll speak to the principal about your 'backtalk' and attitude.'"

An hour or so later, we got to the hospital. They gave us the good news that Weed's surgery had gone well, and I nearly jumped with joy.

"Ready to go back to the farm?" I asked him.

He shook his head with a small, sad smile. "Like the doc said, my recovery is going to take some time and I'm going to need help from a professional physical therapist. Since it's just the two of us, they're not going to discharge me until they're sure I can look after myself." He took my hand and squeezed it. "I know how much all of this has upset you, but we're just going to stay positive and think good thoughts."

I squeezed his hand. I wanted to cry but didn't. "I don't like it at all. Those kids...they just want to fight and yell. They talk about people named Madonna and Britney Spears and Lady Gaga." I paused. "Who *is* Lady Gaga, anyway? Is she a teacher at our school? She must be really good, if everyone's talking about her. I hope I get to take one of her classes."

Weed pursed his lips and stayed quiet for a bit. He looked older now, much older. He seemed older, too. I had always thought of him as a tall, gray-haired kid. "Groovy, I want you to listen to me, and I want you to try not to hate me."

"I could never *hate* you, Weed." Still, I had a feeling he was about to tell me some things I would hate hearing.

"I believe, Groovy, that all people belong to the human family." He caressed my hands as he spoke, but he looked past me, at the wall, as if the words he wanted to say were written there. "I love the life we have built together, but I was a fool to think it would last forever. You're very young and I'm getting very bloody old. I knew perfectly well that our time at Rosemead was limited, but I acted as if I had no hurry to get you ready for the real world. Well, that time has come." He swallowed hard. "You're right, Groovy—that cold, hard world out there isn't very kind to gentle souls like us. I really wanted to ease you into that world nice and slow, but it's too late for that now."

Weed and I had read and talked about old age, loneliness, depression and death, but I thought such things were other people's problems. Now I had to deal with some of that nasty stuff myself.

"This is such a bummer, Weed. It freaks me out."

He squeezed my hand. "Don't be afraid, Groovy. Keep telling yourself, 'I am beautiful, no matter what they say.' Keep loving yourself and be proud of who you are. Remember that you were named Groovy for a reason."

I smiled, even though I didn't feel too happy. "You've taught me well. I know all the stuff that's in the textbooks. I know that I'm smart enough to do the school stuff—but dealing with those kids in that place? It's like I can't understand any of them."

Weed nodded. "I knew this would be difficult for you. You're in another world now, one that doesn't understand you any better than you understand it. We're always freaked out by people and things we don't understand. Yet you need friends—lots of them."

I stuck out my chin. "I have *you*, Weed. You're the only friend I need."

He shook his head. "You need friends your own age. I won't be around that much longer, and we both need to accept that, even if it's a difficult and painful fact for us to live with."

"No. I'm already fed up with people my own age. I've just spent a whole day at a middle school, and it was *such* a drag! Those kids don't want to learn, they just want to make fun of each other and fight. At the end of school, two boys punched it out in front of everyone like it was the normal thing to do! The fight was all about something called 'eyeballing.' Everyone seemed to stand there and cheer for the kids who were fighting. I guess 'eyeballing' is a bad thing."

Weed let out a little sigh. He probably knew plenty about eyeballing, fighting and the rest of the ugliness in the cold world out there. "You just have to pity them," he said, caressing my hands some more. "They sound like very angry people who don't like themselves very much. They'll fight anyone, anywhere at any time. Maybe they'll outgrow it, maybe not."

"Do you know what lockers are?"

"Yes."

"Well, they've got zillions of them at school," I told him. "They said, 'You need to put your stuff in there and make sure nobody can get at it because they'll steal your stuff.' Well, why can't we all share? Why do we need to say, 'This is mine, you can't have it'? Why can't we just love one another and share?"

"Like we did at Rosemead," he said, his voice soft.

"Right on!" I could hear my voice getting louder.

21

"At school, you have to be in a certain room at a certain time. Then the bell sounds fifty-five minutes later and you have five minutes to get to the second class. That place is not about learning and knowledge and education. It's all about being here, then rushing off to there, all before the bell rings. That's way too lame for me."

We heard a knock at the door and watched as Mrs. Davis stepped in. As a former resident of Rosemead, she knew what a righteous place it was and could understand my eagerness to return.

"Weed," she said, "are you feeling any better?"

"Long time, no see, Christmas." Mrs. Davis was pretty, so Weed took a minute to have a nice long look at her as she stood there blushing. "Glad to see you've done so well since your parents sold out and became squares," he added.

They spoke for a few minutes about her parents and some of the other Rosemead people who had come and gone when that farm was the place to be in the late Sixties and early Seventies.

Their conversation seemed pleasant enough, but Weed kept calling her Christmas, and each time he did so, her face sort of changed color and she smiled in a tense, stop-calling-me-that kind of way.

Soon, she said goodbye and took me with her. Unfortunately, we went to her house, not Rosemead. Her house was all on one floor, and most of its floor was fake wood. Also, her house smelled of fake pine and roses. I had grown up smelling *real* pine and roses, so I could tell the difference right away. I could also tell fake wood from real wood, and before arriving in Mrs. Davis' house I really didn't know that fake wood existed. At Rosemead, our house was all wood because that's all there was. Mrs. Davis' house had so many materials I couldn't identify, but that was OK—it was her house, not mine.

Mrs. Davis lived here with her son, Stefan. Now, of course, they had *me* till I moved out, whenever that might be. Stefan didn't appear to be altogether thrilled to have me as a housemate.

"Mom, have you wigged out? Why did you bring that creature here?"

"Please, Stef, lower your voice. You'll hurt her feelings."

"And how about *my* feelings? You bring home Little Miss Woodstock and you expect me to say, 'Yea, Mom! Way to go'?"

"She's all alone."

"Then send her back to the Haight-Ashbury," Stef said.

"She's not from the Haight, she's from Rosemead, where *I* used to live."

"Haight? Rosemead? Who cares? One hippie dope fortress is the same as the others."

"Shush! It's only going to be for a few weeks or a month, until I can find somewhere more permanent for her."

"Oh, so you're making *her* problem our problem, too?" Then, "A month, you say? In case you haven't noticed, I have an image and a reputation to protect. My friends now are total A-listers. They are the coolest of the cool. Do you know how long it's taken me to convince those snobs that I am worthy of their friendship? What will they think when they come over here to hang out with me and they see what's-her-name sprawled on the sofa, watching *Easy Rider* on cable TV?"

The crazy thing was, Stef and I hadn't even yet been introduced to each other. I first spoke to him when I went in search of the bathroom and ended up in his bedroom instead. He was on the phone with someone and his face was all shiny, as if he'd just run fifty miles and was bathed in sweat.

"Git! Go!" He took the phone away from his ear. He made an awful face, to show how mad he was.

"Why are you sweating so hard?"

"It's not sweat, dummy. It's for my face—to keep the zits away."

"What are 'zits'?"

He laughed and shook his head. "Just wait a year or two. You'll find out."

I nodded and left his bedroom. I thought he was the handsomest man I had ever seen. I paid little attention to physical beauty because I had seen few people due to my isolation at the farm. But I did know good looks when I saw them, and Stef had 'em. This was the first time I had ever seen someone who was physically beautiful, and even though he was really mad at me, his attention was...flattering.

My first day outside of Rosemead had been very eventful. I wondered how day two would be.

5

From the mind of…
EUGENE HOROWITZ

ALL GROWNUPS ASK themselves, and each other, "Why are kids the way they are?" The big companies do every kind of research to find out what the kids are spending their guilt money on.

Despite all that research, they don't even know what they don't know.

If you want to figure out kids our age, follow the trippers. No, I don't mean people who go on trips; I mean people who stick out their feet to make others fall on their faces. Trippers are trippees. I know plenty about kissing the floor that way.

Unfortunately, I've always been one of the trippees. Storm Beeson, Gabe Reeder, Heather Marcus and their clique hassle many people here at F Minus, but I'm definitely their favorite target.

Or at least I was.

Now it's Groovy Freedom.

Even a nerd like *me* could bully someone like her and get away with it. I would never do such a thing, you understand, if only because if I did mistreat someone, it would mean that I was no better than Heather, Storm and their stuck-up friends. But Groovy? She was unbelievable.

She was not your average nerd, dweeb or geek. She didn't even wear glasses or have a pocket protector.

She didn't immediately join the science or chess club. She knew zero about Klingons or *Star Trek*. If you said, "Tell me about Harry Potter," she would reply, "I haven't met him yet. Does he go to this school?" Yes, from the moment you first saw her, you knew that there was a new outcast in F Minus, an outcast who had no idea of what happens to outcasts at our school.

So, many people eyeballed Groovy in the cafeteria as she sat down to eat lunch. At least now they weren't eyeballing poor old Horror Wits (that's me). I went over and said hi to her. She would need every friend she could get, and I was about the only one here who had nothing to lose by making friends with her.

"Are you Groovy? I'm Eugene from civics class," I said. She nodded and frowned, as if she'd just been hit with some new information and was trying to take it in.

"Yes," she said after a minute or two. "I've seen you already. There are so many names and faces here to learn."

"You don't have to learn them all," I told her. "But there are some people here you should stay away from." I nodded to my right. "See those kids? They're Storm and Heather. They're sitting with some of their friends and admirers. Not far away are some other kids who really want to become part of Storm and Heather's circle of friends. They think they own and run F Minus, and as far as you and I are concerned, they *do* own this school. Stay away from them. If they pay any attention to you, get nervous and walk away. Also stay away from the druggies, skateboarders and everyone who wears an F Minus white cap."

"What's wrong with wearing a white cap?" she asked.

"Depends on who's wearing it. You can buy a white cap in the student store, but don't do it. You kind of need to *earn the right* to wear a white cap at school, and if you haven't earned it, some kid— especially one who's wearing a white cap, too—will come along and snatch it off your head. He'll then throw it into the garbage or out the window because you've contaminated the cap by wearing it without having *earned the right* to wear it."

"They're pretty caps. They would go nice with my blonde hair," Groovy said. "If I wanted to wear one, how would I go about 'earning the right'?"

I sighed. "If you have to ask that sort of question, you wouldn't understand the answer."

"Oh."

"By the way, where did you go to school before you came here?"

"My Uncle Weed homeschooled me."

"For real?" Our school district had this program, Home Study Option—HSO—where the student shows up once a month for ten minutes to get his textbooks and assignments, then does all his work at home. I had known a few HSO kids, and they all went that route because of the bullies. When you're so afraid of the punks and sadists that you puke up your breakfast on the way to school...well, maybe it's time you went HSO.

"How did you like homeschooling?" I asked.

"It was *out of sight*!" She beamed.

"Lucky you. Must have been nice, waking up each morning, knowing that no bullies or snobs would be waiting for you that day. No trips for you."

"No trips. Weed used to do that when he was younger, but he says you don't need acid or anything else to become enlightened. A person just needs to be high on life."

"Hmm." I was pretty sure I didn't understand one word of what Groovy had just said, but so what? I watched as she ate her lunch—spinach salad, dill pickles, orange juice. She probably ate that kind of rabbit food every day, and that was why there was no fat on her whatsoever. Except on her chest, which was where it was supposed to be. I noticed that she wore no bra. I tried to quit staring.

"What is that you're eating?" Groovy asked.

"A bacon cheeseburger."

She crinkled her nose. "Smells awful."

"But it tastes yummy. Ever had one?"

She shook her head. "I'm a vegan."

"A *what?*"

"A vegan. It means I don't eat animal products of any kind."

"Why do that?" I asked.

She shrugged. "It's just our thing, man."

Just then, I saw a paper ball sail through the air in our direction. I knew who had thrown it, at whom and why. The thrower, Heather Marcus, had tossed it at me but would have been happy to see it hit Groovy, too. The reason for the throw was to say, *We're here, goofballs, and we're watching you.*

They were, indeed, and their paper ball struck Groovy on the head, right where her hair was thickest and heaviest. She didn't notice; she just kept tucking away her rabbit food.

At Heather's table, they hooted and guffawed in celebration of her perfect hit, even though her victim hadn't felt any of the impact. From experience, I knew that the others in their table were getting ready to throw paper grenades, too.

One of the most important laws of life here at F Minus: When the bullies start throwing stuff at you, you *never* retaliate in any way, especially if they're just throwing paper balls. If you throw stuff back or give them backtalk, they think you're challenging them to a fight and therefore it's OK for them to beat you senseless. I've seen four bullies, very slightly provoked, take on one victim, and the victim ended up in the hospital. Naturally, the victim made sure not to snitch on the boys who'd done the tap dance on him. They would just rough him up some more.

Suddenly we heard the voice of Mr. Epperman on the school's public-address system. "Remember, the election for Grade Eight president will happen next Tuesday. It is open to all Grade Eight students. Thus far, we have only one nominee: Groovy Freedom."

I looked at her, my eyes wide. "Are you *really* running for that job? You just got here!"

She looked back at me. "Who was that man? How come we couldn't see him?"

"A better question would be, 'Why is Groovy Freedom running for Grade Eight president?'"

"I'm *not* running. I don't believe in presidents or prime ministers or politics or private property."

"But Mr. Epperson just made that announcement—" I figured it out then and looked over at Storm and Heather's table. They all sat snickering and pointing, and I knew that one of them had put Groovy's name in the box. Some bullies had pulled a stunt like this last year. They had gotten Simon Lummler elected. A shy, pimply computer boy,

Simon tried to live up to the honor. He failed. The kids in the cliques booed and jeered him as he stood at the microphone, trying to say presidential things. By the end of the year, poor Simon felt so degraded and humiliated that he was a no-show at the graduation ceremony. Then he transferred to another school district so he wouldn't have to deal with any of the cretins who'd tortured him at F Minus.

Now we were the Grade 8s, the kings and queens of the hill, and our bullies would pull the same stunt. Only now they wouldn't do it to me or any of the smart, dorky kids. No way. This year they had someone absolutely irresistible, a kid who was such a misfit and outcast that she didn't even think to ask, "How do I fit in?"

I wanted to scream, "Groovy! Get over to the administration office and tell them you don't want to be president! Run, don't walk, and do it right now!"

But I didn't do that. I didn't do anything at all. And the reason I did nothing was that I knew the bullies would simply do to me what they were now doing to Groovy. I knew that the bad guys would nominate me and threaten me with death blows to the brain if I refused to serve as president. Then, as I stumbled through my presidency, they would strip me of my dignity the way the bullies had messed with Simon Lummler's mind.

So I said nothing and kept munching away on my bacon cheeseburger, wondering what would happen to Groovy Freedom this year and if she would be able to cope with it.

At least they would lay off *me* this year.

6

MY DAY WOULD arrive. Soon. It was just a feeling I had.

Very soon, Storm Beeson would become my boyfriend. Yes, he'd been drooling over Heather Marcus—all the boys did, and some of the girls, too. But I knew that Storm would start to sense that Heather lacked my intelligence and earthiness; besides, Heather had the hornies for Gabe Reeder and a couple of the others. Gabe could probably have her, if only removed that goofy ear stud that made him look *so* gay.

Heather was my best friend.

I found it difficult to compete with her. She had natural, fresh-faced good looks, a killer bod and that special quality people call "charisma." Heather told me what she wanted, and she expected me to get off my butt and go get it. Also, Heather once said, "Everyone is either my friend or my enemy," so I wanted to stay friends with her. Being her enemy would be a very bad thing indeed. Being her friend meant that I got to spend lots of time with Storm, and that was just too cool.

Who would have guessed that the most unpopular kid in school could help me to get closer to the man I

31

loved? No, the misfit was not Eugene Horror Wits, it was Groovy Freedom.

As soon as I hurled a paper grenade at Groovy, Storm said, "Good arm. I like your motion." Then he asked me to share my candy bar with him. At that moment I knew he could be mine. We would bond, and maybe even fall in love, over persecuting that flower girl.

We immediately went to work on getting Groovy elected as Grade 8 president. At first we wanted Horror Wits, of course, but Heather insisted that it be Groovy. So I started putting up posters and trying to make everything look official. Mr. Epperman didn't appear to realize that the election was really just a great big practical joke. Groovy appeared totally confused by it all and seemed quite unaware that she just say, "But Mr. Epperson, I don't want to be the president," and that would be the end of that. We could then get Horror Wits, of course, but that wouldn't be nearly as great as the fun we would have at Groovy's expense.

Storm and I worked closely together. We smiled and giggled at each other, and Heather wondered what was so funny. She would have gotten jealous, but Gabe Reeder was always close by. As long as some guy was hitting on her, Heather was happy.

Storm was awesome. We put up all the posters, threatened the lives of a couple of boneheads who said they wanted to run against Groovy, and...done! Our girl was in!

"It's too good to be true," Storm said as we stood in the main foyer. "Heather loves it, too. She said, 'At least Horror Wits would have been prepared for what was going to happen to him. But this girl? Oh, man!'"

He threw back his head and laughed. "Just wait till she has to *look* and *act* like a president in front of the whole school!"

I thought maybe that Storm had read Groovy wrong. If she was new to all of this—public school and a student election—she might not realize that it was all a practical joke. She might take her presidency seriously and do it well. No fun!

When the principal called the assembly to announce the winner of the election, Gabe and Storm lifted Groovy onto their shoulders and paraded her onto the stage. She had been a student here for a little while now. Many of the students at F Minus knew her name from the posters. They had seen her in the hallways. But now everyone was figuring it out: GROOVY FREEDOM, the name on all the posters, belonged to that weirdo hippie girl! Of course! How could it have been anyone else! And now she was the prez! Hundreds upon hundreds of kids gawked at the smiling, blushing thirteen-year-old as if she were some oddity behind glass at Ripley's Believe It or Not.

Groovy, in her own way, was cute. Pretty, even. Tall, long blonde hair, pale blue eyes, milky complexion. Better than decent chest. Take her to the Gap, Banana Republic, Old Navy and dress her up? Hey, she'd be a knockout.

Everyone started calling for Groovy to speak, so Mr. Epperman gestured for the crowd to hush up, then he handed the microphone to our new prez. She stared at her audience for so long that we thought she was stoned.

"I don't deserve this honor," she said finally.

More silence.

"Accept the honor!" someone yelled.

"I don't know you," she said.

Like Obama had to know the voters before he represented them in Washington. Students screamed with laughter at the sight of this hippie waif who didn't know what to say.

I felt thrilled and excited—I think. We had gotten President Groovy elected and let everyone get a good long look at her. Best of all, I had done it all with Storm, and the better I got to know him, the more I liked him.

"That was terrific, huh?" I said as soon as all of the other kids had left the assembly.

Storm slipped his arm around my waist, which I liked, and began half-dragging me towards the stage, which I didn't like.

"Our fun continues," he said through gritted teeth.

Storm's eyes bore into mine. His were even bluer than John Travolta's.

"She says she doesn't know anyone. Well, we can fix that, starting right now."

Before I could think of something to say, Gabe hustled me up to Groovy, who stood by the stage and adjusted her peace-sign headband. I felt badly for her, because here she was, the new kid, the victim of a cruel practical joke, laughed at by so many people. I felt so glad to be popular. I had never been the butt of anyone's joke, but I had seen some really nasty jokes played on some very sensitive kids, and at times I actually felt some of their pain.

"Groovy! Congrats! Or should I call you Miss President?" Storm shook her hand and offered her his meanest little smile. "I'm Storm and this is Erin. Now you've met us, and soon we're going to start introducing you to lots of new people. Isn't that nice?"

"I guess." Groovy really had no expression, except maybe of exhaustion. She certainly didn't seem ashamed, humiliated or degraded. If that's what Heather wanted—and I was sure she wanted exactly that—Groovy had given her no satisfaction.

"I'm bad with names," she said. "I've never had to remember people. It's always been just the two of us."

"You've got all kinds of time to learn lots of people's names," Storm said.

"There's only one name I've ever needed to know," Groovy told us.

"Which name is that?" I asked her.

"Weed."

"Who's Weed?" I asked.

"My uncle. He's about the only person I've known all my life. I don't need to know anyone else."

Groovy had an earthy sincerity that told me maybe we had picked the wrong kid to humiliate this year. I had a hunch that her uncle had raised her to be one tough kid. If Heather, Storm and I had set out to throw paper balls at her, make her our president in that ridiculous election and then put her on stage for everyone to laugh at, the joke was on us—it certainly was *not* on her. We tried to ridicule her; she refused to feel ridiculous. We tried to humiliate her; she chose not to feel humiliated. She accepted the presidency with a quiet dignity that I had to admire. I wondered if she was putting *us* on as much as we were putting *her* on.

Heather continued with her plan, which centered

around Groovy, and I continued with my plan, which centered around Storm. In the library, we installed a suggestion box for students to bring up issues they believed the president needed to deal with right away. Groovy had no idea the suggestions were all nonsense that Heather and I had thought up during lunch hour.

Heather, Storm and I spent way too much time teasing each other and laughing at Groovy. But we had *so* much fun howling at the image of our new president going up to Mr. Epperman and telling him that the students wanted the Coke machines on campus to be adjusted so that the sodas would be free instead of costing a buck each. Additionally, the students wanted a famous rock band to perform a noontime concert each school day so that everyone could enjoy some music while eating lunch.

From what I could tell, Mr. Epperman seemed to have a sense of humor about President Groovy and her recent election. He mostly ignored the issue of student bullying, which was why the Grade 8s last year were able to get away with torturing that kid Simon Lummler. But now our principal had to listen as President Groovy said, "The students want to drink free sodas as they eat lunch and watch Justin Bieber perform. Can you arrange this?"

I'm pretty sure Mr. Epperman didn't say, "Groovy, we need to sit and have a talk about your new job as Grade Eight president—what it *is* and *isn't...*" I don't know why our principal didn't explain these facts of life to our prez, but he didn't.

Thus, our fun continued. Heather said, "Groovy, you need to hold a weekly briefing for the staff of the *Minut Minute*."

"Never heard of it. What is it?"

"It's our campus newspaper. They need to know what's happening so they can report to the rest of us."

Privately, I said, "Heather, what about the *Minute* staff?"

"What about them? I'm sure they have better things to do than attend this briefing. It'll just be Groovy, you, me and a few of our closest friends." Adding, "Those geeks on the newspaper staff? They should be grateful that I didn't make *them* run for president."

Heather scheduled the first briefing that existed only in her imagination. Groovy walked up this hallway and down that one, checking door numbers and scratching her head.

We told her we'd have another briefing the following week. We added that it was too bad she'd missed the first one.

"Bummer," she said. "I'll do better next time."

Our next briefing was in the janitor's closet, which was always locked. Groovy tried the door again and again, and knocked on it till her knuckles nearly bled. Storm, standing next to her, took out his cell phone and called Heather to come up with some of the other cheerleaders. The girls arrived and chanted, *"Prez, Prez, President Groovy! More entertaining than a Hollywood movie!"*

I liked it when the actual press briefings began. Heather even showed up in her regular clothes and brought a palm-sized voice recorder as she and we asked Groovy the questions that demanded answers.

"Miz President, what do you propose to do about the awful food for sale in the cafeteria?"

She shrugged. "I don't know anything about it.

I've never eaten in the cafeteria. I bring my lunch from home."

"Miz President, the boys' and girls' locker rooms stink real bad. How can this situation be improved?"

"You know more about it than I do," she replied. "I would welcome your suggestions."

"Miz President, the school buses need new air conditioners. What are you going to do about that?"

"I don't like school buses either." Then, "I don't have any ideas about these things. Maybe you've elected the wrong president."

We all smirked at each other. Groovy was becoming an even better president than Horror Witz would have been.

Heather wanted to intensify our persecution of the new kid, so I came up with an unoriginal but usually effective prank: I got her a secret admirer. His name was Ronald McDonald, and he deposited romantic notes into her locker.

"Too awesome," Heather said. "Only thing is, what if she likes girls instead of boys?"

"Then I'll invent a *girl* who's in love with her," I replied.

Heather, on Groovy's first day, had taken the new girl to her locker and shown it to her. Therefore, Heather had Groovy's combination, and had given it to the rest of us. We wanted to surprise Groovy by putting something icky in her locker, and when Storm found a small dead garden snake outside, he knew it would be just the item to freak her out in major ways.

Groovy didn't scream when she discovered the small, lifeless serpent in her locker. Instead, she wrapped it up in Kleenex, took it outside to the garden and dug a small, shallow hole.

Storm and I followed her outside.

"What's she doing?" he whispered.

"Burying the snake, I think."

"Why?"

"Gee, Storm, I don't know. Why don't you go ask her?"

So we stood there and watched for a few minutes as Groovy put the Kleenex-wrapped snake into the hole, filled it in with dirt, then patted it smooth. Although I wanted to feel nothing but scorn or contempt what I was witnessing, I instead saw so much compassion and gentleness in Groovy that it reminded me of my gran's funeral, when my family treated her dead body—and each other—with such tenderness and respect on that day. My family members disliked each other, and after the funeral they started fighting again. But on that one day, they managed to overcome their differences. So there I stood, watching Groovy show deep, heartfelt kindness...to a dead snake.

I knew I should have stayed there by Storm's side and shaken my head in disgust at Groovy. But I didn't. Instead, I went up and stood near her as she prayed for the soul of that dead snake. Myself, I hated snakes—to me, they were cobras and mambas and kraits that killed everything in sight. I believed that the only good snake was a dead one.

"Whatcha doin'?" I asked her.

"Saying goodbye," she replied, wiping the dirt on her tattered jeans.

"Friend of yours?"

"All of God's creatures are my friends."

Even Storm, Heather and me? I wanted to ask. Girl, if *we're* your friends, you sure don't need enemies.

"Be well and enjoy your journey," Groovy said to the departed serpent.

By then, some of the other students had stopped to try to figure out why President Groovy and I were standing at the garden, both of us looking mournful and staring at the ground. One kid kind of tuned us in and took off his baseball cap, while another one crossed herself. I looked behind me and made eye contact with Storm, who scowled and shook his head. I silently cussed at myself for letting him down, but at the same time I had shared something special with Groovy, and I did not regret that one bit.

I stood there with Groovy and silently promised her that once Storm became my boyfriend, I would become as unselfish and compassionate as she was.

As I departed, some of the kids approached Groovy and expressed their condolences for her loss. She thanked them and asked them questions about themselves.

7

From the mind of…
MRS. DAVIS

I DROVE OUT to Francis Minut Middle School to meet with Mr. Epperman and find out how well Groovy was adjusting to her new life in public school. Mr. Epperman suggested that we talk while we have lunch, so we did.

"Groovy? We have no concerns about her academic progress. She can do every kind of mental work. I know her background has been very unconventional, but whoever has been teaching her for the past decade or so certainly knew what they were doing. She's one of the fastest learners in our school."

I thought of Weed. I wanted to roll my eyes and cringe. I wanted to tell the principal, "His name is Weed, and he was the only teacher at Rosemead for years. I was one of his students, and he was the toughest so-and-so I had ever met. If you think F Minus teachers are hard cases, you should meet Weed. He said he didn't believe in authority, but he sure loved all the power he had over us. He would have made a terrific cop."

But I didn't say anything, of course.

Mr. Epperman had more to say: "Despite her academic performance, her social adjustment has been disappointing. As far as doing normal, everyday school things, Groovy is completely ignorant. I've never seen any student who dresses so oddly and seems so disoriented by everything. Is she the only student you know from Rosemead?"

"No," I said. "There was one other girl." He didn't need to know that I was referring to myself.

"Does Groovy really believe that we can get Justin Bieber and Britney Spears to play noontime concerts at our school?"

"*What?*"

The principal nodded. "She spoke to me about it as part of her duties as Grade Eight president. She seemed very sincere and businesslike. She had no idea of how ludicrous she sounded."

Grade 8 president! I thought. How did that happen? Wasn't the president elected by his fellow students to represent them? Why would they elect someone like Groovy?

It baffled me until I spoke to my son.

"Mom," he said, as if explaining the punch line of a very funny joke that had sailed right over my head, "being elected is a curse. It happens all the time to the most unpopular students. The first time the F Minus kids saw Groovy, they said, 'Yeah, she's our fool.'"

"Stefan! What a nasty thing to say!"

"What's nasty is that you're a professional social worker and you put Groovy into F Minus. How could you *not* know that those little snots were going to eat her alive?"

"Did this sort of abuse happen when you were in Grade Eight?"

He chuckled. "Oh, it happened—but not to *me*. Do you remember Tori Kathmos? She told everyone she was going to study in Europe for a few months. The truth is, she got checked in to a mental hospital because she couldn't cope with all the mean things people at school were doing to her."

"Were *you* doing mean things to her?"

He shook his head. "But I stood there and watched while the kids reduced her to tears, and I never once said, 'You should treat her the way you want her to treat you.' If I had stepped in and tried to defend her, they would have laid into *me*."

I felt so sorry for Groovy. It was difficult enough for her to deal with Weed's injury and the possibility that he would never again be well enough for the two of them to return to Rosemead and enjoy whatever time Weed had left. Worse, Groovy had been deposited into a school where she had no friends and so many of the other kids were mistreating her for their own amusement. They had no conscience about the impact their harassment would have on her, and I wondered if they ever would develop any empathy.

I reminded myself to be optimistic about Weed's chances for a full recovery. If that happened, he and Groovy could go back to Rosemead. End of nightmare for them. The F Minus kids would then have to find somebody else to pick on. I guessed that task would take them about two minutes, if they really took their time about it.

Also, I told myself that F Minus, on its worst day, was still much better than Rosemead on its best day.

Rudeness, I believed, was a relative concept. Groovy had to come home each afternoon and tolerate Stef's rudeness. He hated Groovy with an intensity that freaked *me* out.

Groovy was different, *very* different, and Stef hated people who possessed that particular quality. It drove him bananas that she adhered to a strict vegan diet. ("Why can't she eat people food like everyone else?") She was meticulous and he was messy. ("Why does she have to be such a neat-freak all the time?") What enraged him most was Groovy's habit of getting up very early to practice yoga outside.

"Stef! What's her yoga got to do with you?"

"Are you kidding me? What if one of my friends drove by and saw her doing that weird stuff on our front lawn? Word would get around and nobody at school would speak to me any more!"

The following morning, as the sun was just beginning to rise and Groovy lay on the front lawn doing her yoga poses, my splendid son doused the girl with ice water. Then he lit into her with a mouthful of curse words that would have made Eddie Murphy blush.

I concluded that my very handsome, very popular son needed to learn a few things about diplomacy and tolerance. He needed to *grow up*.

Groovy looked up at Stef and waved hello—instead of flipping him off, which was what *I* certainly would have done. Poor girl! She looked like a shivering kitten left out in the rain.

"Mom," Stef said, "it's your own damn fault. You should have found somewhere else for her to stay. And you didn't even ask my permission before you brought her home! So don't ask me to apologize to her."

I didn't. I made the apology myself.

"Groovy, honey," I began as I tried, in a motherly

or auntie sort of way, to dry off her endless hair with a towel that wasn't nearly think or absorbent enough to do the job. "You must try to forgive Stef for acting out the way he did, though I'm not sure he *deserves* your forgiveness."

Groovy just shrugged. "He doesn't like me."

"He's a moody, spoiled sixteen-year-old. He doesn't like me sometimes, either."

"If Stef could learn to love himself..." Her voice sounded dreamy. "He would be one far-out kid."

I didn't know quite what to say to *that*.

"You don't have to be so understanding," I finally said, though I found it incredibly wonderful that Groovy really lived up to her name. "Stef can be rude and mean and hurtful. I hope he'll outgrow it—and soon. *He's* had some hard stuff to deal with lately, too. Stef's dad—my ex—tries to be all things to all people, and he makes too many promises. He promised to take Stef for a driving lesson but didn't show up. I called my ex and said, 'Where are you? Our son is ready to go driving,' and he said, 'It slipped my mind. We'll do it another time.' Stef was heartbroken."

Groovy nodded. "Hard luck."

"When you have lots of people in your life," I said, "there's a good chance that they will hurt your feelings and disappoint you. But I think it's great to have lots of people in your life. That's why God's put us on Planet Earth—to be here for each other."

"I've always had Weed there for me. He's been the only family I've ever needed. I don't know what I would do without him."

8

From the mind of…
GROOVY FREEDOM

OH, WEED, PLEASE hurry up and get well. I want to go home to Rosemead *so* badly.

Throughout my young life, each time the world freaked me out, Weed would sit down with me and tell me what the scene was all about. One time, we went into town to get some things we needed. At Rosemead, we grew our own fruits and veggies but had to buy so many other thing from the squares in outside world. One of our first stops was the hardware store, where they sold the nails, tape and glue that were so precious to us at the farm. We rarely bought new things; we just held everything together with glue, nails and tape until it crumbled into a zillion pieces.

When we reached the hardware store, people with signs walked in a small circle at the front door.

"They're on strike," Weed told me. "Their bosses are trying to make them work for chump change, but they're fighting back." He called out, "Good luck to you!" and they replied, "Thank you!"

We ended up driving into the next town to get our stuff, but on our way back, we returned to the hardware store and Weed shook the strikers' hands.

He introduced me to them, and the two of us held picket signs with them for half an hour.

"If the Man tries to push you around, Groovy," Weed told me on the drive back to Rosemead, "you have to push back. Can you dig it?"

"I can dig it, Weed!"

What I could *not* dig was my current predicament at F Minus Middle School. I needed to get into a heavy rap with Weed now, to get my head straight.

Like being Grade 8 president and going up to the principal about bringing in Justin Bieber or Lady Gaga or Britney Spears to perform lunchtime concerts. I spoke to Mrs. Davis about it and she didn't really *say* anything, but her face changed color a half-dozen times and she pursed her lips the way people do just before they vomit. By then, I'd sat through enough computer classes to understand the Internet a little bit, so I typed in the names Bieber, Britney and Gaga and discovered that they were *very* famous performers who were paid millions of dollars to perform for many thousands of people in huge arenas.

I wanted Weed to explain to me why some kids at F Minus wanted *me* to try getting Justin Bieber and Lady Gaga to sing for us at lunch hour. But Weed was still in the hospital, so I had to deal with this hassle all by myself.

So I did. I walked up to Heather Marcus and said, "I'm not going to ask Mr. Epperman again to hire Lady Gaga for a lunchtime concert."

"I'm sure you did your best," she said, squeezing my hand. Then she walked away, and I could have sworn I heard her burst out laughing.

I began to sense that growing up in a world of

two—Weed and me—had limited me in certain crucial ways. Weed and I had enjoyed some wonderful years at the farm, but he was an old man and getting older. If he was wise, it was *his* wisdom, not mine. I would have to learn things for myself instead of turning to my mentor, best friend and only family member and asking, "Weed, what's this scene all about? What does it mean? Explain it to me…"

Most of the time, F Minus was a bad trip, big and confusing, with crowded hallways and students who often stopped me with questions I could not answer. The latest thing was that some cat named Ronald McDonald had put notes into my locker saying he dug my long blonde hair and wanted to "turn on, tune in and drop out" with me. Why would he write such a note?

My friend and confidant at F Minus was Eugene Horowitz. Of course, Weed had already forgotten more about counseling than Eugene had ever learned, but I had to make do with the only person who had any use for me. We made a point of sitting together at lunchtime every school day, and I looked forward to his advice and answers to my questions.

"Ronald McDonald is sweet on you," he said.

I frowned. "How can he be? He doesn't know me and I don't know him."

"Actually," Eugene said, unwrapping another one of his smelly bacon cheeseburgers, "everyone at F Minus knows you. You're a celebrity, whether you like it or not. But you don't know them." He chewed and swallowed a bite. "Maybe he'll ask you to the Halloween dance. Maybe you should ask him. They do that around here—guys ask girls, girls ask guys."

I shrugged. I was doing that a lot at F Minus. "I've

never heard of a Halloween dance. Tell me about it."

"It's a real big item here," said Eugene. "I've never gone to it because no girl would dance with me, and the bullies might get sick of dancing and say, 'Hey! There's Horror Wits! Let's go bug him!' So they would stick my head into the toilet in the boys' can." He added, "Since you're Grade Eight president, you're supposed to be the boss of that dance, or at least attend the event."

"Do I have to be there? Would I have to dance?"

I again regretted leaving Rosemead. Out there, life was so simple—just Weed and me and the acres of nature. We didn't have to understand people and their ego games and power trips.

Why did my classmates throw paper balls at me? Why did I see a dozen or more students deliberately tripped by other students every day? Why didn't the witnesses report it when they saw tripping? How did that dead snake end up in my locker? I'm quite sure *I* didn't put it there. The lockers were there so that dead snakes and other yucky things didn't end up with people's books and clothes.

Weed always said, "Meditation is the best thing in the world. If you're freaked out, just meditate right there and then so you can get centered properly and turn your bad energy into good energy." But what if, while you're meditating, some bully comes along and rips you off because he thinks you're asleep?

Someone stole my sandals, and that was *such* a bummer. If I had ever wondered why Weed and the others had called it quits with San Francisco's Haight-Ashbury district in the late 1960s and moved up north to Rosemead, a few minutes on the F Minus school bus told me more than I wanted to know. I had to go barefoot for the rest of the day because some clown had copped my sandals, and only then did I learn what a sticky, icky, lame bummer of a floor that school bus had. The rest of the bus was no improvement, either. The kids were too numerous, too loud, too rude. They screamed, slapped each other, threw pieces of food and pounded on the windows. Even the bus driver shook his head at them and their antics.

"What happened to your sandals?" Stef asked when I got to the Davis household.

"Someone stole 'em."

He chuckled. "Why did you take them off?"

"So I could meditate," I told him.

"You should have left them on."

"Next time, I will."

"Groovy, you crack me up."

I smiled, pleased that such a handsome young man would find something good to say about me. I felt badly about Stef's neglectful father and those forgotten driving lessons. I again felt the deepest gratitude to Weed, who had always been there for me to laugh with; or, if I just needed a shoulder to cry on, which I often did, well...he was there for that, too.

I blamed myself for Stef's bad energy towards me. I tried to think of something kind I could do for him, but nothing came up. Well, the one thing I *could* do— pack up and bugger off—was something I couldn't do.

9

From the mind of...
STEF DAVIS

MY MOM IS patient, kind, gentle, good-natured, compassionate, empathic, magnanimous, unselfish and gracious from head to toe.

I love her anyway.

She's the kind of person who would say, "Oh, here's a thirteen-year-old hippie girl who's from that Sixties commune I used to live in. It's just the kid and her old uncle, and he's hurt himself. What to do? Hey! I know! I'll take the kid home to live with me! My so won't mind, and too bad for him if he *does* mind. Yeah, that's the ticket!"

Groovy grossed me out when she came home that afternoon with her sandals gone and all that *crap* stuck to the bottoms of her feet. Her hair looked filthy, and don't get me started on her clothes.

"Mom," I said, "she's been wearing the same outfit for nearly a month."

"No, she's changed. She's put on fresh underwear. It's just that her clothing looks the same."

"Take her to Wal-Mart and buy her some discounted Nikes, too. Someone stole her sandals today. They're probably dangling from the top of the school's flagpole right at this moment."

51

"Don't talk like that," my mom said. "The way those kids are treating Groovy is unforgivable. You need to show her some empathy."

"Oh? And who's showing *me* any empathy?" I retorted. "A friend gave me a ride home and we'd just gotten here when Little Miss Woodstock was cutting filth off the bottoms of her feet. She looked up at me and asked, 'Stef, who drove you home?'"

"And what was your answer?" I asked, not really wanting to hear it.

"I said, 'Oh, I was just hitchhiking and he offered me a ride. Know what hitchhiking is, Groovy? It's real easy: You just stand there, stick out your thumb and someone stops to give you a ride. You don't have to pay them any money and often they'll drive you to wherever you want to go. You should try it some time.'"

"I really hope she knew you were putting her on," Mom said.

Here's the deal: If Groovy Freedom causes even one of my friends to stop liking me, she will die. Not even my mother will be able to save that hippie freak.

If I start dating my crush, Janine Framer—are you listening, God? You want to start helping me with this thing?—Janine at some point would meet Little Miss Woodstock. Groovy always seems to be in two places—where I've just been and where I'm going. She's meditating on the front lawn or taking up most of the kitchen table, crunching away on that trail mix that my mom buys for her. Groovy had even discovered the ultimate mind-dissolving drug— television—and started watching the idiot box with me. We watched my favorite show, a half-hour cable program called *Too Cool for School*, and Groovy had some difficulty understanding that the actors could not see the TV audience, because she kept talking back to them as the spoke their lines.

'Groovy! Zip it, OK?"

But Groovy would *not* zip it.

"Adam thinks Kathy doesn't know he's cheating on her with Joanna!"

"Groovy, watch my lips: They're professional actors playing characters. They're reading lines written by writers. It's all make-believe and let's-pretend. You can see and hear *them* but they can't see and hear *you*. Understand?"

She nodded that she did, sort of. But she kept it up, not yet truly accepting the fact that she could not save those characters from themselves and each other. I thought, 'Hmm…how will I explain *that* to Janine, if she and I ever start seriously hanging out together?'

Well, none of that mattered. My thing with Janine went nowhere fast. I should have told Janine that Groovy was my live-in girlfriend or even my wife. I should have told Janine that I was dying of brain cancer.

Sometimes, if you have a thing for someone, it's better if you don't get to know them. I can't believe now that I went to so much trouble just to hook up with Janine for a little while. What a disappointment! We went out, and for a couple of hours she spoke of nothing except how she was cuter than Britney Spears and Brad Pitt reportedly had awful body odor.

Then, "Oh, did I tell you, Stef? Blake and I are getting back together! We're giving it another try! Aren't you happy for us?"

It also bugged me a lot that *she* could drive but *I*

couldn't, so *she* had to drive *me* home. It's hard to feel like a man when you're sixteen years old and have no license or car.

"What's that sitting on your porch?" Janine asked, pointing at Groovy as I got out of the car. "You should call the cops and get it arrested."

I ignored her

At the porch, Groovy smiled up at me. "Hey."

"Why are you sitting there? What are you doing?"

She shrugged. "Just being."

"Where's my mom?"

"Over at the neighbor's." Then, "We better hurry before she gets back."

"Excuse me?"

Groovy held out my mother's car keys. "Driving lesson. Your dad forgot, but I can help you with that."

I guffawed. "A thirteen-year-old is going to teach *me* to drive? Um, I don't think so." But then I remembered that my mother said Groovy knew how to drive, and pretty well, too.

I thought for a moment. At school, our driver's ed. program was all booked up, and my father had made me the lowest of his priorities when it came to driving lessons and everything else. Plus, my mom's schedule left her barely enough to breathe, much less take me out on the road.

I wanted, more than anything, to learn to drive, have a license in my wallet and to start thinking of myself as an adult instead of a kid who took the bus or bummed rides from people. So, why not get lessons from you-know-who?

For the next while, I did many things I'd thought were beneath me. I got behind the driver's seat as

Groovy Freedom sat two feet away. I obeyed her and gave her zero backtalk. Her unflappable Zen personality made her a very patient instructor. Regardless of how many mistakes I made out there, and I made just about every possible mistake except killing other motorists or a pedestrian, Groovy dealt with it in her own quiet, dignified way. At one point, because of the darkness, I raced up a side street until I realized it was actually someone's driveway.

"Don't sweat it," Groovy said.

But I *did* sweat it, and accidentally hit the gas instead of the brake. We got dangerously close to ramming someone's garage door until Groovy leaned over and cranked the steering wheel so sharply that the car missed the house altogether, lumbered right across the front yard and ended up back on the street.

My heart pounded so hard that I thought I was going to die.

"Deep breaths," Groovy said. "Get your mind calm and your energy flowing in a positive way."

"I nearly destroyed their garage—"

"*Nearly.* The garage is still there. Don't get bugged over what *nearly* happened."

So we sat there in the car for a moment, and I felt too scared to drive or think or live. Driving a car was a potentially dangerous, even fatal, activity, and after coming close to taking out a stranger's garage door, I thought maybe taking buses and bumming rides weren't so bad after all.

Groovy said, "Let me tell you what Weed told me when he taught me to drive our truck."

"Shut up," I replied.

"Weed said, 'If the driver gets through, the rest will, too.'"

"Whatever."

"Weed knew all about driving. He used to be the shuttle driver who took people from San Francisco International Airport to all parts of the city. That was before he packed up and moved to Rosemead."

I laughed in spite of myself and cruised back home without much trouble. My mom didn't even find out that I had borrowed her beloved Volvo to take lessons from Groovy, who had gotten *her* lessons from Weed, the burnout who had starred in so many of my mother's nightmares.

I must have learned more from Groovy than I knew. Soon enough, I was driving around town with very little difficulty. I even started to think it hardly mattered that my learner's permit had expired and my "instructor" was a thirteen-year-old who was a few years away from *her* first permit.

I drove here and there, stopped for this light and that one, and I started to feel overcome with driver's ecstasy until I recognized the woman pedestrian I'd nearly knocked on her butt.

"God! That was my mom! My life is over!"

Groovy asked, "What's the problem?"

"The problem," I said, my voice laden with sarcasm, "is that I nearly clipped my mom, and I'm driving *her* car without a license! What we're doing is *so* illegal! Wouldn't you say that's trouble?"

"Does she know it's you driving her car?"

Groovy had a point. My mom and I hadn't made any eye contact when I almost hit her, nor she screamed or shaken her fists at us, so maybe we were safe.

"Well, if she does know, I'm in big trouble and you'll be our city's newest and youngest homeless person."

Groovy nodded, and maybe for the first time started to realize that out here she couldn't just cruise on through life playing by Rosemead rules. But I had lost my nerve for that driving session, so I pulled over and Groovy took the wheel. She drove with the skill and confidence of someone who had been driving all her life—which, of course, was exactly the case. She went down side streets and took rights and lefts...and then we were at home. We let ourselves in through the back door and hopped onto the sofa. We were in the middle of an episode of *Too Cool for School* when my mother came in.

She eyed me, then Groovy, then me some more. "What're you two doing?"

I had forgotten that sixteen-year-old boys weren't supposed to like thirteen-year-old girls very much, especially the two sitting on the sofa at that moment. If Groovy and I were staying quiet and respecting each other's dignity, to my mom it could mean only one thing: We were up to no good.

So I scowled at Groovy and said, "Get up and fetch me a Coke."

"Get it yourself," she retorted.

My mother rolled her eyes and walked away, because I had been ordering Groovy around since her first evening with us.

But I had started to soften towards our hippie guest. In fact, as much as I hated to admit it, I occasionally liked the kid now.

10

From the mind of...
ERIN LANGE

TOO BAD THAT Heather told me she no longer wanted to be with Storm Beeson unless he took that gay-looking stud out of his ear.

It's good that she didn't say, "I want Gabe." She could probably have him because even though I wanted him, too, I couldn't compete with Heather if she made up her mind that she was going to have him. Of *course* she wanted Storm. At F Minus, he was a man among boys. He was handsome and athletic. When Heather said, "Groovy Freedom is our girl. She will be our prez," Storm was smart enough to say, "OK." He stole Groovy's sandals, and I thought that was lame.

"It was *not* lame," Storm told me. "She was sitting in front of her locker and had her sandals off. She seemed to be in a coma or brain-dead or something. I thought she was offering her sandals as some kind of charitable donation, so I accepted them and tried to give them to someone in need. I couldn't find anyone desperate enough to want the sandals, so I hung them on the school's flagpole. It was, like, 'Here are some sandals in case anyone needs them.'"

"Maybe." Myself, I thought Groovy's sandals were hideous. They were made of some material I couldn't identify, and they looked ready to fall apart. I knew Storm had done the right thing as soon as I saw Groovy come to school in Nikes.

"Get her over to SuperCuts and Banana Republic and she'll be a decent-looking chick," Gabe said. "I think she's ready for a bra, too."

Yes, Groovy was ready for a bra, and she was already a *very* decent-looking chick, but I hated it that Storm was noticing her, too. I was so in love with Strom's beautiful blue eyes that I said, "Let's do some more!"

I wrote her more love notes from Ronald McDonald. He wanted to meet with her here and there, and Groovy always showed up and waited. I don't know how she felt about it, but *I* would have been thrilled to have an admirer want to meet up with me, and heartbroken when he was a no-show.

One note from Ronald McDonald asked Groovy to wait for him in the courtyard, and she did just that, and because the note really didn't specify a time, Groovy waited and waited.

Storm and I watched and watched from a library window. Groovy sat there in her familiar mediation position, Nikes off, spirit gone to her special place where everything was beautiful.

"Why isn't she throwing a temper tantrum, or at least having a long, refreshing cry?" Storm asked, gently punching the window.

I understood, or thought I did, but I knew that Storm wouldn't, so I didn't say anything. Groovy, deep down inside, was as tough as wrought iron. Storm and Heather and I could all have our childish fun at her expense, but Groovy could shrug it all off and just do her thing because she saw what fools we were and that our idiotic behavior didn't deserve to be taken seriously.

"We made her wait all this time for someone who didn't arrive because he doesn't exist," I said to Storm.

"And *we* waited all this time for a temper tantrum that didn't happen. I mean, why set someone up for a practical joke when it just falls flat? Where's the satisfaction in that?"

I nodded. Groovy Freedom was F Minus's perfect president. We didn't have to threaten her with death if she declined the nomination because she just went along with every indignity we set up for her. The problem was, she acted as if she didn't know that those indignities *were* indignities. We just couldn't seem to unnerve her.

When we told Groovy that everyone expected her to plan F Minus's Halloween dance and we would all be so disgusted with her if everything wasn't absolutely perfect, she stayed cool and said, "I don't know how to do it." They had confronted Simon Lummler with the same do-it-or-else trip the year before, driving him into depression and anxiety as well as an early departure from F Minus.

So, Groovy—perhaps guessing, correctly, that if she didn't put together the Halloween dance, the school would assemble a team to do the job anyway—promptly forgot about the dance. She didn't even attend the event. I would have been amazed if she had.

Storm got mad because Groovy missed the dance. "She wouldn't have even needed to rent a costume. She comes to school in the weirdest outfits every day."

She and I had one class together—civics. She didn't raise her hand, but when called upon, always provided the right answer.

Storm said, "Groovy is the dumbest kid in the history of F Minus." Wrong. Storm was a shoo-in for that dubious honor. Heather, too.

For friends, Groovy had only Eugene Horowitz. Each day, the two sat together and had lunch. Horror Wits talked and Groovy listened. She doubtless asked him about everything that happened to her each day and told her what it all meant. But Horror Wits was almost as clueless about F Minus as Groovy.

"She's made friends with him," Heather noted as we sat at our preferred cafeteria table and stared at the two pariahs several tables away. "I wonder what they talk about. Probably how it feels to be loathed by everyone." She laughed at his own malicious humor.

Groovy did meditation at her locker, which went over very poorly in middle school. Groovy spent much time centering herself at her locker or strumming folk songs on a school guitar in the music room or doing yoga on the school's front lawn.

"Why were you doing that yoga stuff out front?" Heather asked, sneering. "People will think you're weird."

"Too bad for them," she replied.

In private, Heather said, "I'm going to bug her till she runs screaming and crying to Epperman. That's my goal now."

"Why don't we just bug Horror Wits instead?" I asked.

"Because," she told me, "Horror Wits isn't the prez. Besides, with him, I would just have to get Storm to throw him against the wall and say, 'Next

61

time I see you here I'm going to beat you senseless.' Horror Wits would drop out fifteen minutes later. No, that would be way too easy. Groovy is playing hard to beat, so I'm just going to have to bend her till she snaps."

I didn't like Heather when she got mean like that. Her face changed colors and her eyes got cold and ugly. What if she got mad at *me* for something? Would she try to bend me till *I* broke, too?

"We're seniors," Heather continued. "We're at the top of the heap this year. I'm not going to put up with anything I don't like, and at the top of my list is Groovy Freedom!"

Heather Marcus, Blabbermouth of F Minus Middle School, wanted everyone in our grade to get the message: *Let's bug Groovy!*

Our special thing was tripping, and Groovy was to get the full treatment a dozen times per day. If tripping wasn't possible, a hard shove would do; the main thing was to make sure she ended up on her face or butt. During lunch, paper grenades would be a great idea, too. Everyone should make every effort to persecute Groovy, especially on the school bus, which was where so much student persecution happened.

So, how did Groovy react? Well, she didn't. The tripping worked for a little while, but then she started dancing and skipping around the outstretched feet completely, and she was very agile. At lunch, the paper grenades missed her as often as not, and she appeared to accept them as a part of normal life at F Minus.

Her *fear* was what we wanted to see and smell. But she just didn't have any. She had grown up on a hippie farm where there was no fear, only love and nature and food. Having learned nothing of fear, she didn't know she was supposed to react with fear, even when nasty kids were trying to knock her on her butt.

For me, the weirdest part of all this was that while everyone was cheering on Heather's efforts at provoking Groovy, I secretly wanted Groovy to get back at all of us in some way. Heather disliked Groovy for being different—and I hoped that, when all this was over, Heather would learn a lesson or two, or three, about the problems of having an attitude when it came to dealing with people who were, you know, different.

11

From the mind of...
EUGENE HOROWITZ

THIS WAS TURNING out to be a terrific year for me. My grades were perfect, I kicked everyone's butt at noontime and afternoon chess, I was still the weakest, clumsiest kid in gym class, and I was in no danger at all of getting a date on Saturday night, much less becoming anyone's boyfriend.

But there was something special about being me that year. Something very special.

Everyone I feared kept forgetting I was there.

Every day was as magical as Christmas, and every night seemed like New Year's Eve. I walked the hallways of F Minus and nobody—*nobody*!—would hassle me in any way. Their abuse was already reserved for someone else.

That someone, of course, was Groovy Freedom.

I liked her a lot, and she liked me, too. But she endured so much torment intended for me that I could just go to school, do my thing and enjoy life.

I felt so happy most of the time, but knew that Groovy was getting as much torture as Storm and Heather could give her without getting suspended or expelled. I could tell that Storm and Heather—mostly Heather, the bigmouth—had ordered all of Grade 8 to pick on Groovy.

Of all the times Storm Beeson had gotten his kicks by kicking me—and punching me, slapping me and threatening to spread my big Jewish nose all over my pimply face—this was the first time he'd ever flexed his muscles so much as a bully. That hippie girl had really threatened him in ways he couldn't comprehend.

I wanted to help Groovy but knew I couldn't. I had been Storm Beeson's victim for many years. The teachers and principal wouldn't do anything about it, especially if the bullying happened off campus. Storm Beeson and his jock/jerk pals were *my* problem for as long as they wanted to hassle me.

Now they were Groovy's problem, too. They were her problem because she wouldn't cut her hair, swap her bellbottoms for normal Levi's and replace her tie-dyed T-shirt with something Heather Marcus found acceptable. If Groovy insisted on offending the Big Woman on Campus, well, they would do to her what the Grade 8s last year had done to Simon Lummler.

If you wanted to drive a student bonkers, the school bus was the place for that. In the school itself were teachers and other staff who, if they caught the bully, might actually punish him. But the school bus? Hey, our driver was Mr. Ortiz, a fat retiree who feared the rowdy little buggers and wore earbuds to shut us out. The girls could have danced nude in the aisle, and the boys could have passed around a smuggled bottle of tequila, and Mr. Ortiz would have ignored it.

An item came flying through the air, glowing and smoking. "Hey, Groovy," I said, "they're lighting paper balls on fire and throwing them at us."

She frowned. "Why are they doing that?"

"Because," I said, "they're idiots."

Then Mr. Ortiz went, *"Ohhhh!"* He grabbed at his chest and fell to the floor.

"Ortiz is down!" I yelled.

"Heart attack, maybe?" Groovy asked.

"Yeah. My granddad had one. I know what they look like," I told her.

"The bus is still moving!" Groovy jumped out of her seat and hustled to where Mr. Ortiz lay. Stepping over him, she took control of the big yellow machine.

"Hospital!" she shouted. "Where?"

We sat there like mute quadriplegics.

"Hospital!" Groovy repeated. "Tell me!"

Erin came running up the aisle. "Turn right!"

Groovy cranked the wheel. She got us around the corner and sped up the next street.

"Groovy! This is crazy!" I yelled. "You can't do this!" But then I realized our options were mostly zero and Groovy was simply doing what needed to be done.

She grabbed the gearshift, pulled down and hard, and we went even faster. I wondered what a traffic cop would have thought if he'd seen us—a school bus exceeding the speed limit, cutting off other motorists, horn blasting...and behind the steering wheel a thirteen-year-old girl!

"Groovy!" Erin hollered. "Make a left!"

She did so, a sharp left, and many of us tumbled out of our seats.

I climbed over some kids and reached Mr. Ortiz. "He's still alive. Still breathing, anyway."

Then we heard the radio burp and snort to life. "This is dispatch. Zero-five, how do you hear me?"

Groovy ignored it, probably because she had no

idea what a two-way radio was.

I grabbed the microphone. "Zero-five here."

"Ortiz? We've had reports about your progress the past few minutes and need an update."

"Mr. Ortiz is…unavailable," I said.

"Who's driving?" the dispatcher asked. "Who's speaking?"

"I'm Eugene Horowitz," I told the dispatcher. "The driver is Groovy Freedom. We're students."

"Where is Ortiz?"

"Right here. Unconscious. Heart attack, I think."

"Stop immediately! What's your location? We'll get an ambulance."

"Negative," Groovy said.

"Driver says 'negative.'"

"A student must not drive the bus!"

Groovy pointed at the radio. "Shut it off. He's a bummer."

I shrugged. "Later." I hit the OFF switch. "Groovy, are you sure about this? We're breaking, like, half a dozen laws."

"Weed taught me to let my conscience be my guide. I'm feeling right now that I'm doing the right thing, so this must *be* the right thing, even if the laws say it's the wrong thing."

Some kids in the back row screamed, "Cops! Lights flashing! Busted!"

I heard a deep booming voice from outside. "Pull over immediately."

"Better pull over, Groovy," I said. "Those cops aren't playing with you."

Groovy said nothing. She maintained her speed and frowned, looking from left to right. No cop was going to tell *her* to pull over. Someone or something called "Weed" had told her to do what she believed was right, and she wasn't about to listen to the cops when they told her, "Don't do what's right; do what *we* tell you to do."

As the journey continued, I recognized our surroundings and knew that Central Valley Hospital was just a few miles away. But we had many police vehicles on our tail, and their drivers did not know, or maybe did not care, that our thirteen-year-old driver was trying to save a man's life. The kids on board sat quiet. Some of them were punks, bullies and troublemakers who dreamed, and even bragged, of shoplifting, vandalizing and whatever. But they now sat in that school bus, paralyzed by fear, wondering what the cops would do to them once this drama concluded.

Groovy steered us into the emergency entrance of Central Valley, the hospital in which many of had been born. White-coated staff glowered at Groovy and me as half of the city's police cars pulled up alongside us.

"Need help!" I yelled as soon as the bus's doors opened.

"What's happening?" asked an ambulance attendant.

"Have a look."

The man saw Mr. Ortiz and called for a stretcher. Soon they carried away the old bus driver, and along came a cop.

"Step out of the bus," he ordered Groovy.

She did as told, and he shoved her against the side of the bus and handcuffed her.

"You have the right to remain silent," blah, blah, blah.

As the cop stuffed Groovy into the back of his car, we started objecting.

"You can't treat her like that!"

"She just saved someone's life!"

"You can't arrest anyone that young!"

The cop shook his head and rolled his eyes. "Be quiet and listen! An officer will drive this bus back to school. Nobody make a sound while the officer is driving. Understand?"

The police car drove off and took Groovy away. I felt sure she would endure her trip to the police station with her usual dignity, but *I* felt like crap about the whole thing. Mostly, I felt bad as I asked myself the question, "If she's gone, will those bullies at F Minus start laying into *me* again?"

12

From the mind of…
GROOVY FREEDOM

I THINK THE main reason I actually started to learn about school at F Minus was that I watched *Too Cool for School* on the cable channel as often as I could.

Stef loved it. He knew all the characters and their hangups. Imagine if you attended a high school where all the students were too good-looking. They were really smart and said funny things. Their parents had way too much money and spoiled the kids rotten.

What if your biggest problem in life was being *way too cool*?

Well, that was *Too Cool for School.*

Stef and I sat on the sofa watching that show on afternoons when I wasn't taking over the school bus after the driver had a heart attack, driving to the hospital and getting busted in front of the ER.

As Weed used to say, "No good deed goes unpunished."

When I lived at Rosemead, we didn't have a TV. That had to do partly with conserving electricity, but it was also because Weed had watched more than his share of "the idiot box" and said it lived up to its name. Still, I loved watching *Too Cool.* Each time the show began, I instantly forgot where I was, and who I was, and what my hassles were. I let myself become part of the *Too Cool* world. They were so true to life—and beautiful and stylish!—as they sorted out their issues and made big decisions. I often asked myself, "What would Weed say to them?" Unfortunately, they had no Weed for a heavy rap—neither did I, for the time being. Those TV kids had their parents, who were too caught up with their BMWs, designer wardrobes and vacation plans to bother with relating to their kids. *Too Cool* showed me what life was about in the world outside of Rosemead—vast, complex, full of people who were completely, totally all about ME ME ME ME ME. Also, when their rap gets heavy and they have to make a big decision, the show stops for a few minutes so they can tell you about a new cream that prevents zits forever or a toothpaste that will make the prettiest girls and cutest guys want to kiss you.

The TV show made it easier for me to understand why everyone who was an adult reacted a certain way to my driving a school bus across town to the hospital. The grownups on *Too Cool* went ballistic a lot—that was the TV kids' word, "ballistic"—and so I sat there and let my spirit fly off to its special place while the adults—police, bus company boss, school superintendent, F Minus principal and Mrs, Davis—went ballistic on *me*. Then they put Weed on the phone, and I nearly cried with happiness at the sound of his deep, wonderful voice.

"They want me to give you what-for about driving that bus and saving that man. But all I can say is, 'Right on, Groovy!'"

"The cops are mad at me," I told him.

He laughed. "Too bad for them. The cops say, 'It doesn't matter what's right or wrong. What matters is

71

the law.' Well, when the law is wrong, you have to do the right thing."

"I hear ya. The cop threw me up against the side of the bus and put his knee against my back. Then he handcuffed me."

"They've done the same thing to me. I've demonstrated against wars and gotten a faceful of mace. I've had batons swung at my head. I've been handcuffed many times and dragged into police wagons. Part of living in a free society is saying to the Man, 'This is a free country and I won't let you turn it into a police state!' Sometimes you have to yell that message or they won't hear you. That message is called 'civil disobedience.'"

"It wasn't much fun, Weed. I was scared to death."

"I know, Groovy." Weed paused. "Being brave and doing the right thing is often difficult and scary. Just standing there and doing nothing is much easier. But don't worry. I'm getting stronger every day and soon we'll go back to Rosemead. It'll be just like it was before."

"Promise?"

"Promise."

I wanted to ask, "When we go back to Rosemead, can we get a TV set and get hooked up for cable? I want us to watch *Too Cool for School* and then rap about it afterwards."

I had been doing yoga as far back as I could remember. Weed had been doing it all his life and told me that if everyone did it, the world would become a much safer, saner place.

This was my first day back at F Minus following my adventure with the school bus. I was mostly finished with that day's yoga session when Erin took her place next to me and did as I did.

"Stretch it out," I told her. "You need better extension."

She nodded and obeyed. She did yoga well, very well.

"Sorry," I said, "but I have to go. Heather wants me to do another press briefing. I'm not sure where the room is, so I need some extra time in case I get lost." Then, "At those briefings? They keep asking me things I can't answer. I wish I had all the answers so they wouldn't be disappointed in me."

Erin looked down and said, "Groovy, I think maybe there's something I should tell you. It's about Storm and Heather and me…"

I smiled. "You guys have helped me a lot. You've told me to learn people's names and stuff."

She shook her head. "We weren't being nice. We were picking on you, actually. We keep picking on you. We're not through with you. Be careful." Then she got up and ran indoors, as if she'd just wet her pants or something.

I showed up late for the briefing because I had to ask for directions and people sent me every which way. But I got there and apologized. Storm, Heather and Gabe were there, of course—plus two dozen other kids. I had an idea that Mr. Ortiz and the school bus had something to do with this improved turnout.

"About yesterday's incident," said a student journalist, a fair-haired boy I did not know. "How did you know what to do?"

I thought for a moment. "Well, Mr. Ortiz collapsed and lost control of the bus. So I took control of the bus and drove him to the hospital."

"About 'taking control of the bus…'" he persisted.

"My uncle taught me to drive a long time ago," I explained. Then, "We've never met. What is your name?"

"David Tomlinson," he replied.

I took out my tattered, pocket-sized notebook and wrote his name.

"How did you know that Mr. Ortiz had a heart attack?" asked a girl sitting next to David Tomlinson.

"I didn't," I said. "But his face was turning purple, so I knew it had to be serious. I just did what I thought was best."

"My name is Randi Katman," she said.

"Spell it, please." She did, and I wrote it down.

A tall boy at the back asked, "What did the police say to you?" Then, "Neil Kowski." He spelled it out. I wrote it down.

I thought for a moment. "He said, 'You better watch your step or you'll end up doing time in a youth facility.'"

"Didn't you tell him that you were trying to save the bus driver?"

"No, I just walked as carefully as I could."

Heather snarled at me and shook her head. I didn't know why, because she had insisted on these briefings as soon as I became president.

"Why is it," she wanted to know, "that you haven't even begun organizing the Halloween dance that means so much to this school?"

They had begun advertising the dance throughout the school. Heather was correct in saying that I hadn't done a thing to put it all together, mostly because I didn't even know where to start. But I still had a very strong feeling that I had lots of helpers I didn't even know about, and my helpers would make sure that the dance would be very beautiful.

"It's true that I haven't started on the dance," I said.

"Shouldn't it be one of your top priorities as our president?" she asked, smirking.

"Yes, but—"

The bell rang just then. I wiped some sweat from my upper lip as the students filed out of the room. David Tomlinson waited till everyone left, then approached me.

"First thing you need for a party," he said, "is a disc jockey. I know just the guy—he was trained by Kaskade and he really knows how to keep the kids freakin'."

I understood very little of what he'd just said, except that a dance needed music and someone to play it, preferably someone who knew what he was doing. I remembered that Weed once told me about how, when Rosemead was a commune in the Sixties, they always gave the biggest jobs to those who the most qualified. So why was *I* in charge of the dance when I had no idea of what one looked like?

I said to David, "About music—do you think the kids would like dancing to the Grateful Dead?"

"The Grateful *what?*"

"Maybe *you* should deal with the music."

His eyes lit up. "You want me in charge?"

"I don't like putting it that way," I said. "I grew up believing that no one should be 'in charge' of anything. There should be no bosses. You're just the

75

music guy."

He nodded. "OK, I can get us a great DJ who has his own music. But he won't do it for free. Who's gonna cover his fee?"

"Too bad we live in a money economy," I said. "There's a line from the New Testament: 'The love of money is the root of all evil.'"

"The school sets aside money for a dance DJ," said Randi Katman, who'd stayed behind with David Tomlinson. "It's in their budget. Right, Groovy?"

"If you say so." Back on the farm, Weed used cash to pay for things we absolutely needed, but I had no experience with money at all. So I told David just to go ahead and make sure we had music for the dance. I assumed that was the right thing to do. If it wasn't…well, what a bummer.

13

LITTLE MISS WOODSTOCK was turning out to be someone I could tolerate. Not long after my first driving lesson, my dad came by, all smiles and handshakes. His job involved much travel, even to different parts of the country, but he said he'd stay put for the next several months.

"I know you want to get a driver's license, Stef. Let's work on that, now that I'm going to be in the area for a while."

"Stef was heartbroken when you canceled your first lesson with him," my mother told him.

"It's OK, Mom. Now that he's here and I'm here, we can go driving," I said, wishing she would shut up and go away.

"Yeah, son, let's go driving,"

So that's what we did. My father lacked Groovy's patience, of course, but ever since that school bus incident, our hippie houseguest hadn't gone near a vehicle.

At the conclusion of our session, I eased his Taurus up the driveway.

"Who's that?" he asked, pointing at a figure on our lawn. "Is she the homeless kid your mother brought home? What's she doing?"

I nodded. "That's her, and she's doing yoga."

"Does she have to do it outside so the whole neighborhood can watch?"

"I guess she likes doing her yoga outside in the fresh air. Don't ask me why."

"How much longer will she be here?"

"She'll be here till she leaves," I said.

My dad let out a small, bitter laugh.

My parents were very different people. My mom was so nice, kind, patient and generous that she inadvertently made most of the people in her life—especially me—feel like selfish creeps. But my dad came along and understood exactly why I disliked Groovy. Oversimplified, my mom drove away my dad by caring about everyone else as much as she cared about him. He couldn't accept that; he needed to be a *very* special person in her life—*the* very special person—which he was not and never would be.

My dad and I had always gotten along, maybe because we were a lot alike, or because we were different in all the right ways. He worked too much now, traveled too much, and I missed him too much.

He waved and smiled at Groovy. "Yoga, huh? I used to do karate, years ago." That was Dad, being nice to someone he disliked. A career salesman, he had mastered one of the key rules to making sales: Become whoever you need to be in every situation.

Groovy said, "Karate is nothing like yoga. Karate is a martial art. It's about violence."

To me, my dad said, "Must run now, but here's something I think you'll really like." He took a small box out of his pocket and handed it to me.

The box contained a heavy gold chain.

"I know these things are very popular with guys

your age right now, Stef."

He was right—this was the year of bling for boys. A heavy gold chain around your neck looked way cool. Plus, this one was real gold, not fake.

Groovy's jaw dropped open. "That's so fine. Wow!"

My dad laughed. "It's OK, I guess. You probably haven't done much shopping in jewelry stores."

"I've never been to a jewelry store. What's in it?"

"Stuff like this," I said, pointing to the chain.

My dad pointed at Groovy. "Yeah, you're from Rosemead. Stef's mom grew up there. It was quite the place back then. It got press writeups from all over the world. What's happening there now?"

Groovy told him far more than he wanted to hear, mostly about the fruits and veggies they grew there. Dad listened and nodded, then rolled his eyes at me in such a comical way that I nearly burst out laughing.

Welcome home, Dad!

14

From the mind of…
GROOVY FREEDOM

WITH SOME EFFORT, I had managed to memorize a couple of hundred names and faces. But I still had so many more to go.

Weed had always told me, "Don't let the bastards grind you down." Of course, he meant the *real* bad guys in Washington, D.C. and Wall Street and all the other places where they cared about nothing and no one except stuffing other people's money into their own pockets. But I knew he meant that I should protect myself against bad guys everywhere.

As time went on, more students came up to me and introduced themselves. I wrote down their names right away, and they started asking me questions about the time I saved the bus driver's life. They seemed largely uninterested in Mr. Ortiz's well being; they wanted to know why a person becomes a hero, especially when they know that their heroic deed is very illegal and can get them into tons of trouble.

I ran it down for Weed during one of our phone conversations.

"Being a hero is against the law, Groovy," he told me. "It's been that way for a long, long time. Our society is all about power, profits, private property, punishment and prison. Those kids you go to school with? Their parents say to them, 'Don't get out of line or the cops will come along and throw you in jail.'" He sighed. "In many ways, most of the people in the straight world are in prison. You can't get out of prison until you realize that you're *in* prison."

"Stef Davis," I told him, "is so totally on this trip about getting his driver's license."

"Yes. I mean, what *is* a driver's license, anyway? It's a plastic card with your name and picture on it. But the thing is, the Man says you can't have a license till you're sixteen. It's all rules, regulations and laws out there." I heard him sigh. "So you did some underage driving to save someone's life, and the kids are all saying to you, 'Hey! You broke the law and got busted for it! How did *that* feel?'"

Weed was so wise. I wanted to call him two dozen times each day. I was full of confusion, full of questions...and he was full of answers and common sense. But the best we could do, for now, was to talk on the phone.

"Weed, are you improving? When will they let you out so we can go back to Rosemead?"

"The doctors say I'm improving. While I'm doing my thing, you need to keep doing yours—and that means loving yourself and doing what's right. Over there at F Minus, it sounds like they're on a race to the bottom. You need to make sure you stay away from that race. I've never met Stef Davis, but I remember his mother, Christmas—she really didn't want to learn the lessons that Rosemead had to teach, and maybe Stef is his mother's son in the wrong ways."

"Weed, aren't you being negative?"

"I suppose." He sighed some more. I had heard him do that much too often since our crisis began. "It's this rehab center. It's such an institution, and you know how I feel about such things. It reminds me of why I left San Francisco to move to Rosemead all those years ago. They keep calling me Mr. Levenson! I hate that! I'm Weed!"

My heart broke as I listened to Weed. He was letting the bastards grind him down. I had seen that happen a handful of times in my entire life, and the thing that soothed him and cooled him out was getting back to the farm.

Weed spoke ill of Stef without ever having met him, but that was because most of what Weed knew about Stef was the bad stuff I had said. Stef did have his good moments. We had spent many afternoons on the sofa watching TV and talking about it later on. Stef was very handsome and had a terrific smile. I couldn't think of Stef without thinking of *Too Cool for School*, because in many ways I thought of him as one of its characters. He may not have been aware of it, but he liked the show so much because he related so well to the beautiful, narcissistic young people who acted in the show.

Stef had what the movie business called "presence." I had studied art with Weed throughout my young life and thought of Stef as a piece of art. I wondered which beautiful woman he would marry and if she could put up with him as well as I did.

Seth mellowed some once his father got back and their driving sessions were going well. Mr. Davis was a nice enough guy, and he did his best to appear that he was happy to see all of us, including me. Mrs. Davis looked really lonely much of the time, and when I saw them together, I thought it was pretty clear that he had left her and she sort of wanted him back so that she wouldn't be so lonely anymore. I wondered if he got lonely the way she did, and what he did about it. Maybe loneliness was different for men and women.

I thought about these things long and hard, and I decided that as soon as Weed got out of that awful rehab place and we went back home to Rosemead, he and I would sit and rap for hours about all the things I had witnessed and experienced. I was so full of questions that sometimes I thought I would burst.

Plenty of people started speaking to me every day, mainly about that Halloween dance.

One afternoon, I watched *Too Cool for School*. Most of it was set at a school dance, so I figured out quickly enough what the F Minus kids expected of me. The TV kids made like they were fighting on the dance floor. They bumped their bodies together and pumped their fists into the air. I thought, *So this is what they've been bugging me about? It doesn't look like much fun. It looks like one of those riots Weed was in years ago.*

"I think we need food for the dance," I said. "On *Too Cool*, they ate stuff between dances."

"Yes," said Ariane Burnell. "They need snacks and drinks. Energy food so they can dance longer. Pizza and Coke are great ideas. They're convenient, too. Just provide lots of paper towels because pizza is so greasy."

"Oh." Then, "Well, can you do that for us? Pizza and Coke?"

She nodded. "But it's going to cost some money.

83

Pizza worth eating is fairly expensive."

"Do it," I said. "I'm sure the school can come up with the money." In reality, I wasn't sure of that at all. But as Weed would say, "If it's someone else's problem, let *them* worry about it." I would let the school worry about paying for the snacks.

"Out of sight, girlfriend!" Beaming, Ariane ran off to do her thing.

Right after that, someone drew up a list of all the jobs that needed to be done for the dance. Within fifteen minutes, every job had a volunteer.

15

GROOVY'S PAL.

That's what they called me. I didn't mind, of course. It was a better deal than being called "Horror Wits," which I disliked a lot. Yeah, I was more than OK with "pal."

Also, the word fit. If Groovy had a *pal* or *friend* at F Minus, I was that person. She had many *acquaintances* but I was her only *friend*. Those two words, *friend* and *acquaintance*, have very different meanings, but people get them mixed up all the time. They say *friend* when they mean *acquaintance*.

Anyway, Groovy and I spent many hours together—but our hangout time happened only at F Minus. Then she got on that big yellow bus and headed off to that social worker's house to watch cable TV with Stef, the good-looking, bratty son. I think she was starting to like him a little bit more, or hate him a little bit less. She seemed to like him the way girls liked boys. Groovy was a girl and I was a boy, but that didn't matter in our friendship. I guess I was starting to like girls, but Groovy was way too different for me to like her as a possible girlfriend, and I was way too nerdy and ugly for her to have a crush on me or anything. So we just kept on being friends, because nobody else had any use for either of us.

"Join some clubs," I said to her. "You like chess? We play every Wednesday afternoon."

"That's competitive, right?" she asked.

I shrugged. "We play matches against each other. If you play against someone who's better than you, you'll probably improve."

"So it's about winners and losers," she said. "I'm not into that. I hate it that someone has to lose."

"Want to come over to my house and watch some TV?"

"No, thanks." Simple as that.

"Why don't I go to your home and watch TV with you?"

"Negative. It's not my home. Stef might be mean to you. I never know with him."

"Want to go to Westside Mall?" Then, "That T-shirt is awesome. It has every color in it. Where did you buy it?"

She tugged at it. "Weed and I tie-dye our own T-shirts at Rosemead. Do you want me to show you how?"

"Would you?"

She would, and did. We met in the art room before school. She told me to bring a couple of plain white T-shirts, so I went to Wal-Mart and bought the cheapest three-pack they had, so that if I botched up the tie-dyeing process despite Groovy's help, my loss would be minimal. But I needn't have worried.

"You need to scrunch, twist and tie them like this, then put rubber bands on them."

86

"We sure have a lot of chemicals here," I said, pointing at the paints, dyes and solutions she had found in the cabinets.

"We need it all to create beautiful shirts," she said.

We had just started dipping a T-shirt into a tub of purplish liquid when the art teacher, Mrs. Tunnicliffe, entered the room to begin preparations for the day.

"Groovy," I whispered, "did you get permission for us to do this?"

"Permission to do what?"

"Eugene Horowitz!" the teacher yelled. "I don't remember giving you permission—" Then, "Say, aren't you Groovy Freedom? Mr. Ortiz is back home and feeling better, thanks to you!" She looked into our tub and exclaimed, "Hey! Tie-dyeing! That's *so* much fun!"

When her first-period class showed up, they found her with Groovy and me, all three with purple-stained hands.

"There's been a change of plans," she told them. "Clay is tomorrow. Today we're tie-dying, as you can see. Go to your lockers and get a T-shirt or gym shorts and bring them in."

Mrs. Tunnicliffe, as a courtesy to us, called down to the principal's office and had us excused from first period. Moments later, the announcement blared over the public-address system: "All students wishing to do tie-dyeing with Grade Eight President Groovy Freedom may do so in the art room…"

Far too many F Minus students wished to do tie-dyeing with President Groovy. Mrs. Tunnicliffe laughed out loud with delight at the sight of so many who were so interested in what was happening in the art room.

At the center of it all, Groovy helped each person who needed assistance; she dipped this and scrunched that with the deftness of someone who had been tie-dyeing since birth. Which was probably the case with her.

When things quieted down a little and the kids had completed their tie-dyeing, they asked Groovy some more questions about her school bus heroics and her progress in organizing the Halloween dance. They paid the closest attention to what she told them, and I realized then that while everyone at F Minus had seen her at the assembly and in the hallways, none of them could truthfully say, "Yeah, I know Groovy Freedom."

This tie-dye party had been my attempt at spending a few hours getting to know her better, but it turned out to be President Freedom's post-election reception. The art room was packed for the longest time, and virtually all of those kids made sure they had a personal conversation with Groovy.

She had washed her hands, taken out her well-used little notebook and written down many new names.

F Minus, for most of that day, became a psychedelic trip as countless students paraded around in their tie-dyed shirts and shorts. They laughed, pointed at and slapped palms.

Best of all, nobody threw a paper grenade at Groovy's head or tried to trip her. Nobody.

16

From the mind of...
GROOVY FREEDOM

THE VIBRATIONS WERE bad, very bad, when I got off the bus and walked to Mrs. Davis's house. Her car was in the driveway, which meant she was home early, and that was a downer. Plus, as I got to the door I could see through the window that the TV was turned off. *Too Cool for School* would start in five minutes, but today I might miss it. Double downer.

Stef and his mother sat at their kitchen table.

"This is just a part of life," Mrs. Davis was saying. "You'll just have to deal with it."

"What's the buzz?" I asked. "Tell me what's happening."

"Go back to Rosemead," Stef said, snarling.

"Stef! Mind your manners." Mrs. Davis frowned at her son.

"This conversation is over." He got up and stormed off.

"Maybe I should go apologize," I said.

"It's not your fault, Groovy. It's just that his dad went off again to do some business, and they'd made plans to hang out and do stuff together."

"Father-son outings, huh?"

She nodded. "My ex is a charming guy, but he's such a...*salesman*. He's all smiles, handshakes and promises, but then he forgets all about the commitments, obligations and responsibilities he has. He was a great boyfriend but a bad husband. That's why I called it quits with him. Stef keeps expecting him to mature and grow up and start being the father his son wants him to be. But that isn't going to happen."

I felt badly for Stef. He was so disappointed by his father's broken promises. But I noticed that he wore that heavy gold chain, so now he got to be one of the ultra-cool kids at school. Maybe that made him feel a little bit better. Stef was very concerned, all the time, with how much people liked him. If they wanted to hurt him, they just had to ignore him, and he would hate himself. I had never felt that way about anyone. I didn't need the approval of a chosen few— I liked myself just fine the way I was.

Maybe part of Stef's problem was that he knew way too many people. I was starting to know more and more people, and it could be a bummer sometimes.

I watched *Too Cool for School*, and one of the characters, Shawn, really bugged me. He didn't cheat on his girlfriend or tag buildings with graffiti, but his behavior was so bad that I wanted to crawl the TV screen and tell him some things that Weed had told me about life.

"Don't get all worked up," Stef said, sneering. "It's

just TV. It's make-believe." He was still very bummed out about his dad and all the quality time they *weren't* spending together.

"But if Shawn doesn't study," I pointed out in a very loud voice, "his SAT scores won't be high enough and Stanford will turn him down."

"Well, what of it?"

"He's not taking the SAT seriously enough," I said. "He's hardly cracked the books and he sleeps in when he could use that time for more useful things."

"That's the point of *Too Cool for School*. The characters are all rich, charming and good-looking. But they're lazy and spoiled. They just want to have fun. They're throwing their lives away, and that's why they're so much fun to watch. If they had their act together, they would be boring."

"But what will Shawn do if he doesn't get accepted into Stanford?"

"What does it matter? They will write him out of the show and the actor who plays Shawn will get a part on another show."

Since Stef had been something of a couch potato for many years and had seen many actors on many TV shows, he cared little about Shawn and would not miss him when Shawn disappeared from the show. I, however, had started to think of Shawn as the tragic older brother I'd never had.

I got upset with Shawn because I was pretending that I was him and his SAT problem was my own. How could Shawn just sit back and relax, smug in the belief that he would have SAT success without working for it? Plus, how did he think he would get into Stanford—an awesome opportunity!—without great test scores?

As Grade 8 president, I had that Halloween dance coming up, and for a while I had done the Shawn thing—forget about it and hope it went away.

For Shawn, everything worked out fine. He crammed for the SAT, did great and got into Stanford. He ignored his problem until the very last minute, literally, then dealt with it—and his problem went away as if it had grown wings and flown off into the clouds.

I sat there on the sofa and thought for a moment about that Halloween dance at F Minus. Like Shawn on TV, I had done a lot of sitting around doing nothing despite being the one mostly responsible for the dance. Its failure would be my own. (But I wasn't sure that its *success* would be my own.) A "committee" had formed around me, and the snacks, drinks, posters and decorations were being worked on. Students would approach me just to say hi; in the music room, when I played and sang, they would turn it into a singalong. They would do yoga with me and then say, "Groovy, you're the prez. What can I do for you?"

So many people were spending so many hours after school working on the Halloween dance that I actually started to believe it would happen and be a success.

It didn't surprise me too much that *Too Cool for School* was such a big hit. Its characters succeeded in spite of themselves. Not unlike the characters at F Minus.

Life at Rosemead had taught me that in order to get veggies, we had to plant seeds and care for the land. No seeds, no care, no veggies. No veggies, no food. No food, starvation. But school wasn't a farm, and students weren't veggies. (Well, maybe a few of them were.) They elected me Grade 8 president, and the Halloween dance was my job. By Rosemead logic, if I didn't do it, it wouldn't be done. But when I did very little to put the dance together, those around me did all the stuff I wasn't doing, and they made sure the dance would happen after all.

Even Weed had to admit there was something righteous about that.

"Groovy Freedom! I need to speak to you immediately!"

I stopped mediating the moment I heard Mr. Epperman's voice. You don't keep meditating when the principal wants your attention.

He glowered. "Why haven't you set up a meeting with me?"

"About what?"

"About?" His face went red. I thought he needed to meditate and get his energy flowing in the right direction. "About fancy pizzas and mobile music services. That's very expensive. Who's going to pay for it?"

I shrugged. "I thought the school had money set aside for those things."

He nodded several times. His face stayed red. "Oh, it does. It *does*. But the thing is, you and I are supposed to get together in my office and create a budget for that Halloween dance. We have to do that budget *before* I can let you spend the school's money on fancy pizzas and mobile deejays."

"I don't have a budget," I told him. "I wouldn't

know what a budget looked like if I saw one."

"Well, if you had come to see me," he said, as if speaking to a very small, very stupid child, "we could have made a budget together."

"Well, I said to the kids, 'I need help,' and they said, 'We'll give you that help.' So all we need is the money to pay for the music, snacks and drinks. I didn't think I needed to bug you about the money. It seemed like such a hassle."

"And when were you going to ask me for the money?"

"Well, back on the farm, Weed would get bills in the mail and then he would pay them. I figured it would sort of work out that way here, too."

Mr. Epperman sighed. "OK, Groovy, I guess you win. The fancy pizzas and the music service have already been ordered, so we can't cancel them. You and I are going to the bank to start a checking account so that we can pay for these things. If you're going to be Grade Eight president, you should at least learn a few things about budgeting and paying bills. You've already learned about delegating responsibility."

Right after school, he drove me to First National. That was my very first time in a bank, and from the moment we entered the place I knew I would hate the experience. Weed said that banks were like churches, except that banks worshipped the Almighty Dollar. Everyone in the bank was dressed in serious clothing. They all acted serious and the man at the door, who wore a blue uniform and carried a gun, was the most serious of all.

I wanted to get *out of there*. I didn't like stuffy places where people were dealing with money, and I definitely didn't like being around men with guns. I had recently met a few of them, and it was a bad scene.

"Relax, Groovy," said Mr. Epperman. "He's a security guard. He's on our side."

Whenever I thought I was over the biggest hurdles when it came to everyday life outside of Rosemead—Mrs. Davis's house, F Minus and all the rest of it—something would come up to remind me that I still hadn't learned where the bathroom was. In fact, I didn't *want* to learn where the bathroom was. I just wanted to get home to the farm and kiss its dark, smelly soil.

Mr. Epperman and I met with a plump, balding assistant manager. We went into his office, sat down for a while, and when we left, I held in my hand a book of checks that, printed at the top, said STUDENT SPECIAL EVENTS.

"These go for the food and music we talked about." Mr. Epperman had already signed the first dozen checks. "Write the checks as the expenses come up. You'll be amazed at how expensive everything is today."

I wanted to explain to him that the pizza guy and the music guy were being dealt with by other students, not by me, so maybe I should just give the checks to the students who would be paying those bills. But he didn't listen. He just went on about how that money in the checking account belonged to all of us, and I should spend it responsibly and set a good example for everyone else.

Unfortunately, I had no clue as to how to write checks, spend responsibly and set a good example for others. I was just a hippie kid from the farm, and all I really wanted to do was go back home with Weed.

Mr. Epperman offered to drive me to Mrs. Davis's house, but I said no thanks. I walked instead, getting the stink of money, cologne, perfume and armed security guards out of my head.

17

From the mind of…
MRS. DAVIS

I LEFT MANY messages for Mr. Epperman, and he finally got back to me.

"Sorry for the delay, Chris," he said, "but I barely have enough time to breathe."

"I understand. I'm calling mainly about Groovy Freedom. Has she been making much progress?"

"Depends on what you mean by 'progress.'"

"Bad news, huh?"

"She could be much worse," he told me. "At first I was afraid she'd be so bullied and mocked that she would transfer out of here immediately. But she's done very well, considering she's such an outsider."

"Has she made any friends?"

"Well, let's just say that she's a 'person of interest' to many of our students. Do you remember when she commandeered that school bus?"

"How could I forget?" I asked, chuckling.

"To some of our students, that made her quite an outlaw rather than a heroine. And kids *love* outlaws, so many of them have made a priority out of getting to know her better."

"So they're not bullying her?"

"Quite the opposite. She held an impromptu tie-dyeing clinic that was remarkably popular. Whenever she goes into the music room to play guitar and sing Grateful Dead songs, many students join her. She does yoga in front of the school, and two dozen other kids decide *they* should do it, too. This Halloween dance? Every kid here wants to help out just because Groovy is the boss, even though she insists there's no such thing as a boss. Imagine if this was 'Sixty-seven in the Haight. I think Charles Manson got started that way, sitting on the street corner, strumming his guitar."

I didn't tell him that back in the olden days, we had a hippie cult leader at Rosemead, and his name was Weed. Groovy had learned most of her life's lessons from that old guy.

"I'm glad you're feeling good about her progress. When I first learned that she had been elected Grade Eight president, I thought, 'How odd! They don't even know her!' Then my son said, 'It's a practical joke,' and I got very worried."

"I was worried, too. In the fairly recent past, some of our student 'presidents' were the least likely to succeed, and they had a terrible time of it, which amused some of our meaner students. But we continued with student government, and this time Groovy seems to have made it work out well. So far."

"So far." I also noticed, and was sure the principal did, too, that Groovy had made little if any effort to conform in her style of dress. The students would have felt less alienated by her if she had started dressing the way they did. But of course, if she had done that, she would have stopped being Groovy Freedom, and there was no *way* she would stop being who she was.

Her refusal to stop being herself also irritated—enraged?—Stef, who, much like his father (and mother), demanded that those around him do their best to gain his approval. Groovy was having none of that. Stef was happy with that heavy gold chain his father had given him. It made him look like a drug dealer. I prayed he wouldn't get his ear pierced, too.

The two could sit on the sofa and watch *Too Cool for School* without trying to kill each other. Groovy, I'm sure, had some sort of schoolgirl crush on Stef, who was handsome and vain and therefore totally fascinating to her.

I didn't know for a fact that there was any sort of romantic interest between Groovy and Stef, but one day when I came home from work I saw the two of them on the sofa watching *Too Cool for School*, that ridiculous series for teens that was on every day. Its main message seemed to be, "You don't *know* how hard life is when you're better than everyone else!" Anyway, a very hot makeout session was happening on the screen—I felt relieved that it was between a boy and a girl and it involved no nudity (you never knew what you might see or hear on *that* show!)—and Stef sat there watching it, his breathing ragged. Meanwhile, Groovy sat there watching *Stef* with absolute fascination. She could be a very mysterious person sometimes, but she was still a thirteen-year-old girl, and I had a feeling she was readying herself for her first kiss. But I was *not* ready for her to start practicing on my son.

I cleared my throat and said, "Well! It's sure hot out there! Who's in the mood for a tall glass of iced tea?"

"Mom!" Stef held up his hand to shush me. "My

show's on!"

I liked to think that I wanted to protect Stef from an inappropriate encounter with Groovy, but in reality, I wanted to save Groovy from being thrown off the sofa if she got too close to Stef. He liked girls just fine—but to him, she wasn't a girl, even though she was getting curvier every day.

I felt badly for Groovy because I had spent years at the farm, then needed to adjust to the outside world. My struggle from Rosemead to civilization had occurred many years earlier, but the memories came back, and saddened me, each time I looked at her. I believed Mr. Epperman when he said that she was making progress, but I was still eager for the day when she would be reunited with Weed and the two of them could run, not walk, back to their farm.

18

From the mind of…
EUGENE HOROWITZ

I WAS THE first to join Groovy for yoga in front of the school, and the first to quit.

Of course, nobody noticed my absence. Nobody cared that I was her best, and maybe only, friend. I couldn't do yoga at all, and the harder I tried, the worse I got. I wore my tie-dye clothing and caught no flak from anyone, because Prez Groovy, my pal and everyone's heroine, had turned me on to it. I hung out with her before she had driven a bus, saved a life and put together a dance.

So I tried to do yoga with the others, and all of a sudden, someone got their leg tangled up with mine and I fell flat on my face. We were on the grass, so it didn't hurt so much as humiliate me, and I'm not sure who did it, but Storm Beeson is the likely one, because he was right behind me. The moment it happened—and I considered it an act of bullying—I got up and left. I haven't been back since.

I wondered if the persecution was going to start up again. Groovy had come along and become every jerk's favorite target, so it was, like, 'Let's not bug Horror Wits any more, because we've found a new victim.' But now Groovy was the closest thing F

Minus had to a celebrity. It started with the school bus ride to the hospital; how could any kids our age fail to respect a classmate who takes over the bus and refuses to stop even when surrounded by cop cars? Groovy was *bad*, and *bad* was as *good* as you could get. Plus, she saved the driver's life, and her whole attitude was, 'Yeah, whatever.' You really have to admire someone who does heroic stuff *but does not brag about it*. After all this, of course, people started treating her with the respect and admiration a Grade 8 president deserves.

Nice for her—but what about me? Did her good deeds and rise in popularity mean that the bullies would start picking on me again? I could only wait and worry.

Of all the people who had boarded the *Let's Hear It for Groovy! Yea!* bandwagon, the person who seemed most unlikely to do so was Erin Lange. She ran with Heather Marcus's clique, and was Heather's best friend. Erin was always ready to participate in Heather's practical jokes and other nasty business. If Groovy was F Minus's president, Heather and her friends were its bosses, even though Epperman and most of the other adults did not know it.

I, of course, scarcely knew Erin Lange, and I wanted to keep it that way. If Heather had said to Gabe Reeder and Storm Beeson, "Go find Horror Wits and try to drown him in the toilet," they would have asked, "Which toilet?" I had heard that Erin had a queen-sized crush on Gabe and Storm, and if *I* knew about it, you had to figure it was the worst-kept secret at F Minus.

So why did she want to spend so much time with Groovy? Erin was the best at yoga aside from Groovy, and often approached the hippie girl to share some Grateful Dead trivia she had heard or to rap about the lessons America should have learned from the Vietnam War. Also, when we had that spontaneous tie-dyeing day, Erin was the very first to show up after they made the PA announcement. I knew that she was at the opposite end of F Minus's campus when she heard about the tie dyeing, so she must have run like mad across the entire school to get to the art room so fast so she could be near Groovy.

Still and all, Erin was a member of our school's elite. So when Groovy and I were standing there as Heather paraded by with Storm, Erin and Gabe, I backed up against the wall so they couldn't trip me.

"Hey, Groovy!" Heather gave a little smile and wave. Her greeting was for Groovy; Heather didn't know I was there, and if she did know, she was smart enough to pretend she didn't see me. "We're doing a walk for charity and we need sponsors."

Storm acknowledged my presence, sort of. He glowered at me. "We need *your* help, too."

I nodded and dug in deep. I pulled a pair of damp dollar bills out of my pocket and handed them over. I didn't believe any of their blah-blah about helping people. What he meant was, *We need money to spend on ourselves, and if you give us some, we will stop bullying you for a little while.*

"That's all I've got," I said as Storm gave the money to Heather.

Heather gazed at Groovy. "Prez, can you help us?"

She nodded and took out the checkbook.

"Groovy," I said, "isn't that the school's checkbook? Like for school activities?"

She shrugged. "Mr. Epperman told me to spend the money responsibly, and I think that charity—"

"Groovy," I said, rolling my eyes, "the money in that checking account is supposed to be for the Halloween dance."

She just smiled. "Dude, have you been inside that bank? I have, and it's just filled with money. I'm sure they'll have enough bread for the dance when it comes time to pay." She wrote the check, tore it off and gave it to the queen bee.

"Prez!" Heather's voice was a very hoarse, emphatic whisper. *"A thousand dollars?"*

"Groovy," I said, keeping my voice calm but feeling every bit as freaked out as Heather. "Negative. You can't do this. Mr. Epperman will trip out when he learns about this."

She shrugged and smiled. "Giving is better than taking. He will feel wonderful about it when he finds out." She added, "Weed always said—"

"What Weed said doesn't mean spit around here," I told her.

But by then many students had noticed the spectacle: President Groovy in a hallway meeting with Heather Marcus and her crew. Something very heavy was going down.

Heather took the check and showed it to all who cared to see.

"You're fantastic, Prez!" she screamed.

"Yea, Groovy!" Gabe shouted.

People clapped and cheered. I shook my head and wanted to crawl into my locker and die. I also wanted to yell, "Listen up! That check has the school's name

104

on it! It's meant for *school* things, not charity! It's not her money to give away!"

Then Groovy pushed through the crowd, slapping outstretched hands and smiling at people who patted her shoulder. I followed her down the hallway.

"You must feel good right now." I meant that as a criticism but was pretty sure she didn't take it that way.

"I feel *so* far out," she said with her big blonde smile. "It's just out of sight to know I've helped so many people just by writing that lame old check."

"Tell that to Mr. Epperman."

Then she let out a big sigh and added, "I didn't know how wonderful it feels to have so many people like me so much. It just makes me feel so high."

I couldn't relate to her at all. For a smart boy, I knew nothing about having friends and being liked. I probably would never know, either. One thing I liked about Groovy was her compassion for Horror Wits the Pariah. That was something we'd had in common…and now she'd become popular. She was rubbing my face in the fact that she was Prez Groovy and I was still Horror Wits. Ouch! What an insult!

We stood there, very close to the boys' and girls' bathrooms. From behind us up came Erin Lange, who threw her arms around Groovy and said, "Thanks for the check!" The hippie kid went red-faced for a moment, then leaned into it and hugged back.

I scowled at her. I now hated my best and only friend.

19

From the mind of…
HEATHER MARCUS

I SAW THIS thing on TV were scientists were trying to figure out how we will know when the end of the world is upon us. Most of them thought there wouldn't be enough water, and therefore not enough food, and starvation would wipe out all seven billion of us. Some of them thought a country would nuke another one, and goodnight.

They knew zero.

I knew that when someone named Groovy Freedom becomes student-body president, and all-around most popular kid of F Minus, then you know we're at the beginning of the end of human life on earth. Groovy is a kid who, when you look at her, you're not sure if she's a chick or a boy. Of course, that's starting to change, and many of the boys are starting to like that fact that Groovy doesn't believe in wearing a bra.

What's really got *me* bugged was Groovy's crappy dance. No, it wasn't crappy, everyone said—it was freakin' awesome.

"Too bad for you," Storm said. "Remember how you told all those kids to hassle her? Well, she won them over and got them to help her organize that dance."

Well, yes. Only Groovy and I stood back and did little or zero.

"This party is gonna *rock!*" Erin stood back, admired the decorations and starting shaking her hips in a little victory dance. "Who doesn't love to shake her booty?"

"The dance is sold out," I muttered.

"But that's *good*, right?" Erin asked.

Gabe laughed. "Heather's mad because this was supposed to be *her* year and it's turned out to be Groovy's year."

"Heather," Storm said, "don't sweat it. Groovy looks weird, and she refuses to conform, but who cares? I'm sure she's going to be remembered as our best prez ever. It's a win-win, you know?"

"No, I *don't* know." I felt a bit embarrassed at how cranky I sounded. Still, I went on. "The Grade Eight presidency was supposed to be a practical joke. We get her elected, she makes a fool of herself, we laugh at her, she freaks out and goes back to Planet Fringus."

"Well, that was the plan," Erin said, nodding. "But Groovy took matters into her own very capable hands. She really lives up to her name. Groovy rules!"

I laughed in spite of myself. "I wonder how much longer Groovy is going to rule after Epperman finds out about all those big checks she's been writing for all those charities."

I wondered if somehow Mr. Epperman knew, and approved, of those checks. Groovy wouldn't be permitted to donate all of F Minus's "student activities fund" without getting the OK from the office. Or would she? Maybe Epperman allowed it to happen as a lesson in good will. I hated that. Our student election was a joke. Our Grade 8 president was supposed to be degraded and humiliated, not admired, respected and permitted to give away the school's money.

I didn't know what Epperman was making of all this, but lately, and because of Groovy Freedom, I had been fighting with my friends and enjoying life at F Minus much, much less.

"My year"? Well, it was *supposed* to be that way. But now I was turning into that good-looking snob who kept on dissing President Groovy.

I was the one who felt dissed when, in the cafeteria, after I paid for my food and went to my usual table, I found *her* in *my* seat! F Minus had a big cafeteria, of course, and there were many other places to sit—but that was beside the point. We, the elite, the clique of cliques at F Minus, had chosen that section as our own, and everyone else needed to respect that. From my first day here, I had recognized that one certain part of the cafeteria had the best view and was the place the A-listers sat to socialize with one another while they ate their crap sandwiches. I sat there because a nearby window sent shafts of noontime sunlight that struck my blonde hair and made me appear to wear a golden halo. That special seat, and the golden halo that went with it, reminded everyone of how wonderful and magnificent it was to be me, Heather Marcus.

Those beautiful rays of sunlight now fell on the unwashed tresses of Little Miss Woodstock. I tried to make contact with Gabe and mouth the words *Tell her to get lost*, but he just looked away. What a wuss! I watched him for a moment and noticed he was staring at the big red EXIT sign, his very subtle way of telling *me* to scram. Erin was busy talking to Groovy, but Storm looked at me. I looked at him. He gave me the tiniest shrug, which meant that I was on my own until they accepted me back into their clique, if *that* ever happened.

I choked down a huge sob—part of being a cool kid is never, *never* show any emotion—and spun around with my tray to find somewhere else to sit.

Bang!

Our trays collided. His food mingled with mine, and mine with his.

He was Horror Wits. His eyes bulged with fear—not of me, but of Storm Beeson, who, at my command, would maim or kill Horror Wits.

"Idiot!"

I had lots more to say, but then I saw his expression as he looked over and saw Groovy—who no longer had any use for *him*, just as my crew had banished *me*.

This was definitely the low point of my life at F Minus. I had bottomed out socially, and there, waiting for me, to keep me company at the bottom, was Eugene Horowitz.

"My fault," Horror Wits blurted, swallowing hard and often.

I didn't feel fondness for him at that moment, but I didn't hate him, either. He reminded me of the good old days, before Groovy Freedom came into our lives.

Eugene should have been Grade 8 president, that was for sure. If Groovy had come along a day later, Eugene would have been elected and Groovy would have been little more than another campus freak.

"Never mind the trays," I said to Eugene. "Let's

sit down and talk."

He swallowed again and shook his head. His face seemed to vibrate with anxiety. I had said vile things to him, and ordered others to slap him around, for as long as I had known him, which was most of my life. So I really couldn't blame him when he thought my invitation for a conversation was just a ruse to set him up for a slapping around or practical joke.

"I want to talk to you about Groovy."

He looked past me, to where she and the others were sitting. He grinned. "You're no better than I am now."

"Guess not."

"I was her friend when no one else would speak to her." He thrust out his chin. "You and your friends have been bullying me all my life."

"Well, things have changed a little bit. I'm out and she's in. It sucks."

Eugene nodded.

"Wanna do something about it?" I asked.

He snarled at me. "*You* suck, too! When has anyone ever said, 'Heather Marcus owns this school'? Why do you get to be everyone's boss? You started all this ugliness when you said, 'I don't like Groovy, the new kid. Let's torture her.'"

"I don't remember seeing you step in when we made her president. You were just glad we were picking on *her* instead of *you*."

"And so you and your stuck-up friends just totally laid into her. How would you have felt if she had been unable to cope with that torture and she committed suicide? Huh? You know what? I don't think you would have cared one bit, because the only person you care about is Number One."

"The only one *anyone* cares about is Number One," I shot back. "Did I—or we—drive Groovy to suicide? No, I don't think so. Look, she's prez, right? That's how it's gonna be for the rest of the year. But maybe we can sabotage the Halloween dance—"

"No! No! No!" His face stayed red and tense. "There you go again! Now you're trying to wreck that dance just because someone has robbed you of some social status."

I looked over to where I used to sit. Groovy and Erin were laughing about something.

"Makes you sick, doesn't it?" Eugene said.

"Yeah, really," I said. "We'll talk again."

"What do you have in mind?"

"I'll tell you when the time is right," I said.

20

From the mind of…
GROOVY FREEDOM

I STOPPED PUTTING so much effort into learning the names of new people and decided to be a better friend to those I already knew. Weed would be proud of how I had done so well on my tests and other assignments, but the truth was, the schoolwork at F Minus was much too easy.

Stef and I started spending few hours together on the sofa watching TV. *Too Cool for School* was no all reruns, and I was fine with that. When seeing it for the first time, I lost track of characters and events because they were all so new to me. The second time around, I could follow everything more closely and put it all together.

"Shawn is still a jerk and Marianne hasn't decided which guy she wants next," Stef said.

He was right. But the *Too Cool* kids were just that, and I easily spent twenty-two minutes ogling them each weekday afternoon. They were good-looking, clever, rich, spoiled. Did such kids exist in real life?

Stef had chilled out some. He looked handsome and dangerous in his baggy jeans, Reeboks, black T-shirt emblazoned with NWA. Also, his heavy gold chain and baseball cap made him look like an MTV video bad boy.

For sure, the best thing about being me was my ability to help the world by writing those checks Mr. Epperman had given me. He didn't know about those charitable donations because he had been at an out-of-state conference or something, but he would get back soon enough. I knew that when I told him about those checks for charity, he would be very impressed. I thought it was weird how money, and its effect on people, had gotten Weed so freaked out that he left San Francisco and went north to Rosemead. Yet, money could do so many things to help so many people live such better lives!

I wanted to talk to Weed about it during our next phone rap. Money could help everyone, everywhere with everything. Wasn't that just too far out? Mr. Epperman's checks had allowed me to reach out and touch people's lives in a very special and beautiful way. It was totally consistent with what Weed, and Jesus, and Buddha had preached.

I felt so eager for the principal to return so that I could show him where the money had gone. Also, I needed some more checks if I wanted to continue my good work.

"We have a pep rally today," Eugene Horowitz told me. "You should be there, Prez."

"What is it?"

"It's a meeting to foster school spirit. The whole school meets in the football field's bleachers so the players can show off and the cheerleaders can bounce up and down and everyone can chant, 'We are the greatest!'"

"How long does it take?"

"A couple of hours."

"Why so long?" I asked.

He shrugged. "Some things take time. Anyway, it's really an exciting event. It's to get us pumped up because we have a game against Hamber coming up and they're our biggest rivals."

"Rivals?" I asked. "What have we done to them?"

"Our teams play against each other every year. Therefore, we are rivals."

Weed and I had never been sports fans, because mostly it involved winning and losing and knocking the other guy on his butt. However, since I was president, I clearly had an obligation to attend this event.

I went with Eugene out of the building along with many, many other students at well before noon. I could hear chanting, cheering and the ringing of bells. My heart pounded and my pulse sped up, although I did not know why. I failed to understand why we should get so excited over our football team and whether it won or lose. I wasn't into winning or losing; I was just into being.

"What do I do?" I asked Eugene. "I'm the president, so do I shake hands and say hi? Is that my thing today?"

"I'll show you." He took me away from the crowd and through a doorway marked LOCKER ROOMS. Then we opened the door marked VISITORS.

"This is for the boys," I told him. "I'm a girl. Haven't you noticed?"

"You're the prez," he replied. "You can go wherever you want."

Eugene lifted a set of pads off a shelf and placed the equipment on my shoulders. "You're going out there in uniform. To support our team."

I frowned. "I'm not a boy and I'm not a football player."

"You don't have to play. You just have to go out there in uniform to show everyone that President Groovy, who's a girl, is a major fan of our football team."

Just then, we heard an announcement blare through the school's public-address system: "Ladies and gentlemen, make some noise for our very own Francis Minut Destroyers!"

I heard many feet pound the cement floor on the other side of the door. The crowd made the requested noise and lots of it. They made as much of a racket as Deadheads at a concert. I respected that.

"We'd better hurry," I said.

"We have time," Eugene said, pulling a blue jersey over my head and past the shoulder pads. Then he put a helmet on my head and tucked in my hair.

"Headgear's too small," I said.

"No, your hair is too big."

The facemask made it hard to see.

"Do I really need to wear this stuff?"

"Yep." He pouted for a moment.

"Are you OK?"

"I'm never OK." Then, "You're all ready to go. Get out there and show your F Minus pride!"

Following his directions, I hurried through a tunnel and felt exhilarated as I got nearer to the sound of cheers. But as I emerged from the tunnel and came into view, those cheers turned into jeers. People booed. They scowled at me and gave me the thumbs-down sign. Some even made obscene finger gestures at me. I spotted the Destroyers and trotted towards them, to show my support. They came to me, too—charging, faster and faster, arms outstretched, and it didn't look to me like they wanted a hug.

At that moment I noticed something odd. We were all wearing football uniforms and protective equipment, but with one big difference: Their jerseys said MINUT while mine said HAMBER. I was wearing an enemy uniform. What was up with *that*?

21

From the mind of…
STORM BEESON

THE HAMBER TIGERS were the team we loved to hate, and that pep rally really helped us get pumped up to cheer on our team as our Destroyers prepared to take on the Tigers. When that kid showed up on the field in a Hamber jersey…well, the crowd ate it up. What a great stunt to stir everyone up! Yeah, we knew that the kid wasn't a *real* Hamber Tiger, and I'm still not sure who managed to snag one of their uniforms, but once the kid showed up, we knew what we needed to do.

By the time Gabe yelled, "Dead meat!" we were in full pursuit of the bad guy.

If I wasn't the fastest Destroyer, I was its best tackler, and I really wanted to strut my stuff in front of everyone who had crowded onto the bleachers. Their cheers and whistles inspired me to run harder and faster than I'd ever run before.

I have to say something now, and I'm not lying. I am as big a liar as anyone, but this is the truth: I had *no* idea who that fake Tiger was, this brave soul ready to be flattened by us just to give our fans a thrill. I assumed person also needed to be a trained athlete who was prepared to take a king-sized hit.

A few moments before I plowed into the kid, I'd gotten close enough to see that this kid had a *chest*. The kid was a *girl!* It was the worst moment of my life.

As I slammed into her, I tried to fling her away so that my teammates would hit *me* instead.

I yelled, "No!"

Too late. My teammates were charging at their target the way a bunch of NFL bruisers would pursue a punt returner. When they hit their target, I heard a horrible *crunch!* that sounded like bones breaking. It wasn't much fun for me, either, because I was at the bottom of the dogpile. But what about the poor thing in the Hamber uniform?

The crowd screamed and cheered with such intensity that I could hear them from under a dozen or so big male bodies.

The F Minus coaches then rushed out onto the field, yanking bodies away one after another.

"What's this stunt all about?" I heard our coach yell. "Whose idea was this?"

I got up and shouted, "Nobody told us about it!"

Coach said nothing as he knelt and eased the Hamber helmet off the mystery kid.

A few miles of blonde hair sprang out from underneath the helmet and vast numbers of people shut up as President Groovy Freedom lay spread-eagled on the football field.

"Groovy," Coach said, "speak to me. Can you hear me?"

She reached into her facemask and pulled out a fist-sized clump of dirt. "Bummer."

Coach and one of his helpers hauled Groovy to her feet and half-carried her off to get medical help.

Some people clapped, but most just sat or stood in shocked silence, as if Groovy had been broken in half.

The crowd stayed quiet. We, the Destroyers, just stood there and watched as our fans left the bleachers, following Groovy in much the way that I had seen mourners walk during televised funerals for heads of state—slow, dignified, respectful.

I turned to my teammates. "Any idea what happened? Who got her to put on that uniform, anyway?"

"Maybe she thought it was a good idea at the time," replied one of our guys. "She wanted to participate in a memorable way."

"No," I said, "she had no knowledge of it. I guess it was another practical joke. This one almost got her killed."

"I think," said Gabe Reeder, "she probably did this one on her own. She does crazy stuff all the time."

Gabe had spoken, and I should have just nodded and said yeah. Heather Marcus had the most influence of any student at F Minus, but many kids would have said it was Gabe, or even me. Whatever influence and power and prestige and I had at school came from my friendship with Gabe. He taught me to believe that I wasn't quite as dumb as I seemed. For me, school was nine months of going into this or that room, sitting for close to an hour, staring at a book or chalkboard and going *Duh*…But then Gabe taught me that school had jack-squat to do with education, knowledge, learning, intelligence and getting As. No, school was about girls and fun and sports and hanging out and having a good time.

119

But Heather had gotten mighty weird about Groovy, and maybe she had been leaning on Gabe to do something like dress up the kid as a Tiger and let us pummel her. I couldn't figure it out.

Coach stormed back right away, his fists clenched. "Part of my job is to teach you something more than the fundamentals of football. Things like 'work together, be good sportsmen and, most important, use your brain.'" He wiped some spittle from his lips. "So I can't imagine why any of you would think it was OK to take out some small kid wearing a Hamber jersey. And that kid happens to be a girl!"

"She gonna be OK?" I asked as Coach paused to take a breath.

He nodded. "But *you*, Beeson—you showed some real hustle out there. More than I've seen from you in a long while. Now, what I need to know is: Who is responsible for talking Groovy Freedom into putting on that uniform so that you could tackle her?"

We all stared at his shoes and said nothing.

"OK," he said, "but Mr. Epperman is going to be back soon, and I'm going to tell him all about this and he's going to ask you about it. When he asks you, I don't think you'll have the option of saying nothing."

We changed back into our street clothes and went back to class, but the pep rally and the Groovy incident hung over everyone's head. All the students had witnessed it and spoke of nothing else. What was it all about? Did the Destroyers know that the prez was in that enemy uniform, and was she going to be

OK?

People talked and lied and made up stuff. Someone said that Groovy, the ultimate peacenik, was going to come to F Minus with lots of guns and shoot us all.

"That's crap," I said. "We didn't know she was in that uniform, and she's not mad. Just shaken up."

"We all need to chill," said Heather. "I understand that she's all right and will be back here for her afternoon classes."

I nodded. When Heather Marcus said "I understand," it was good enough for me. She blabbed a lot and heard a lot, and her information was usually of very high quality.

"I still don't know whose idea it was to do that to her," I told her.

"I do. Want me to tell you?"

"Yes, please."

She mouthed, *Horror Wits.*

"Impossible." Then, "How?"

Heather told me about seeing Groovy in the cafeteria, the clash of lunch trays, the quick plan she'd made with Horowitz.

My face got red. Heather asked, "Storm! What's wrong?"

"That wimp will die," I muttered, walking in the general direction of Horror Wits's locker.

As I got closer to my destination, I noticed that the other students parted for me as soon as they saw me coming. I liked that. As Gabe had said to me so many times, if you can't get their respect, their fear will do just fine. They backed off, and within a few minutes I hustled up to Horror Wits. He saw me, his face went white, and he looked this way and that.

"I guess you know why I'm here," I told him as I dispensed with further small talk and let my right fist do the communicating.

Crack!

Oops!

When my brain cleared up and I could understand my surroundings, I saw Horror Wits still standing there, totally unharmed and laughing at me. At our feet lay President Groovy, who had stepped in to stop me from punching out the fat kid.

"Ohhhhh…Wowwww…." I ran a hand through my hair, disgusted.

The entire hallway rocked with nervous laughter. Kids pointed at me and Groovy and shouted at each other that Storm Beeson had just laid out Prez Groovy for the second time that day.

Not knowing what else to do, I lifted Groovy and carried her to the nurse's office. When we got there, I was still so freaked out that I forgot to lie when the nurse asked me what happened.

"Fistfight," I told her.

"The two of you? Were you fighting a girl?"

"No, she tried to break it up. I was about to punch out Horowitz—"

"*Eugene* Horowitz? You're twice his size."

"Yeah, well…he did something I didn't like."

"So you were going to punch him out…but you ended up punching out Groovy Freedom instead."

I nodded. "Yes, ma'am."

"Storm," the nurse asked, "have you seen a counselor lately?"

She tended to Groovy and sent me to Mr. Epperman's office. Actually, she sent me to the waiting room outside of the principal's office. So I sat there and waited as students passed by, looked at me through the window and made faces or flipped me off. Storm Beeson, football player and all-around tough guy and bad dude, now he's in trouble for roughing up the student-body president, a thirteen-year-old girl. I sat back and sighed. I deserved whatever punishment they gave me.

Groovy had *character* and *substance*. I admired her for that. She was more of adult than I could ever hope to be. she had shown me that, for all my tough-guy bravado, I was really just a scared little boy.

The three-o'clock bell rang and the students began leaving F Minus. The nurse hadn't arrived yet, but the yellow buses had started to arrive to take the kids back to suburbia. But I also saw an ambulance.

An ambulance? Why?

It couldn't be for Groovy because I hadn't hurt her that badly. Plus, the big white emergency vehicle seemed to be in no hurry—it just crept along behind a couple of school buses. But why was it there?

The answer came into view a moment later. The nurse helped puffy eyed President Groovy. The students stepped aside to let the nurse and the kid through. As the two exited the building, the crowd outside parted for them. In a moment or two, they reached the ambulance.

 Indifferent to the consequence of leaving the waiting room without permission, I got up and sprinted out the school's main doors and got as close as I could to the nurse and Groovy. Then I yelled, "Groovy! I'm so sorry! Please forgive me!"

But the nurse just helped him into the ambulance and it went away. I knew we had lost the greatest prez F Minus had ever had.

22

From the mind of…
GROOVY FREEDOM

I GOT INTO the ambulance and was so happy I could have cried. There he was, waiting for me.

He sat up and smiled, looking older and thinner than I remembered, but he was *there*, and that was the only thing I cared about.

"Weed," I said, leaning over and hugging him, "you don't know how much I've missed you."

He hugged back, then held me for a moment and looked at my face. "What happened?"

"Fistfight," I told him.

"Did some bully hassle you?"

"No, it was between two other people. I tried to break it up."

"Your face is going to look bad for a little while, till it heals." He paused. "Bummer."

"Yeah, it's a drag. Now, what's happening. Are we going back to Rosemead, or what?"

"Is that what you want?" he asked, smirking.

"Yeah. I think Mrs. Davis is getting sick of me."

Weed laughed. "And I think that rehab center is getting fed up with *me*. I speak my mind, and they don't like that too much. I told the ambulance driver to come straight here and get you, because I hate this

F Minus place almost as much as you do."

"Oh, it's not as bad as all that."

"You're a forgiving person, Groovy."

We reached Mrs. Davis's house so I could get my stuff. I barged in, calling, "Mrs. Davis! Mrs. Davis!"

"She's still at work," Stef said from his place on the sofa. "What you want?"

"I'm going home."

"I thought you *were* home."

"I mean my *home* home. Rosemead."

Stef brightened up. "For real?" He got up and looked out the window. "That ambulance yours?"

"For the moment."

"I guess Weed is in there. Why doesn't he come in and say hi?"

"He's still mending. Want to go out there and see him?"

Stef shook his head. "Not necessary. My mom used to live at Rosemead. She's told me a hundred Weed stories." Then, "Your face is a mess. Aren't you going to tell me who punched you out?"

"No big deal," I told him. "I just need to get my stuff and I'll be gone."

He helped me pack, and that took about two minutes. Soon there was no trace at all that a hippie had lived with the Davises.

23

From the mind of…
MR. EPPERMAN

MY OUT-OF-STATE trip had gone great. At the conference, they told me about how terrific a job I had done at Francis Minut Middle School, and that a higher-paying job as principal of Valley High would soon be mine if I wanted it.

I felt so good when I flew back home that I believed nothing could bring me down.

Of course, when I returned to Minut, I expected to see many phone messages, emails and other pieces of business that required my attention because I was the boss. But as I riffled through the envelopes from my in box, I kept seeing items from First National Bank.

One of them said URGENT. Inside, a note told me that the enclosed check was overdrawn. The check, one of many obtained and signed by me and given to Grade 8 President Groovy Freedom to be used for the Student Activities Fun, had been made payable to the American Diabetes Association in the amount of one thousand dollars.

Not being a complete dummy, I assumed that all of the other First National envelopes littering my desktop contained bounced checks. That meant we had zero in the account that once had a balance of four thousand dollars. Had Groovy given all of it to charity? What about the dance?

Feeling my blood pressure rise, I instructed my secretary to send Groovy Freedom to my office.

"She withdrew during your absence. His uncle was discharged from the rehabilitation center and I believe they have returned to Rosemead."

"What's their number? Call them and insist that she come in."

"They don't have a telephone."

So, with no options left, I personally called Chris Davis and left messages on her home phone and cell phone. I even sent her an email and text message.

Amazingly, she arrived at my office within half an hour. By then, I had called First National's manager and apologized for Groovy's reckless spending. I had also called the mobile disc jockey, who accused me of "dissin'" him with "rubber."

"Chris," I said, "you understand Groovy Freedom much better than I do. Would you explain these checks to me?"

She looked through the returned checks and bank statement. Her face turned a few shades of gray.

"Bob, I think you're at fault as much as she is."

I frowned. "Me? How?"

"You gave her all those blank checks. Why did you do such a thing? Did you explain to her what those checks *were* for and *weren't* for?"

I let out a huge breath. "Yes, I kind of thought I did. I spoke to her about it and assumed that she had enough common sense *not* to do what she quite obviously did. I definitely did not say, 'Here, Groovy, take this bunch of checks marked STUDENT

EVENTS FUND and make them payable to the charities of your choice.'"

"But you knew that Groovy had spent her entire life isolated in Rosemead. She didn't have the 'common sense' you gave her credit for having."

"Maybe," I said. "But she should have known she was committing fraud."

She shook her head. "Groovy was no more capable of committing fraud than raising John Lennon and George Harrison from the dead and organizing a Beatles reunion."

"Even a kid that age knows you can't spend money that you don't have," I told her.

"Bob," Chris said, "let me tell you a little bit about myself. I was raised in Rosemead, and for all that time, I had scarcely any idea of what money was. I never saw any, never touched a dollar and couldn't have cared less about any of it. The adults were, like, 'Money? Whoo, bad stuff, man.' Then, when I was around Groovy's age, my folks decided that they had had enough of Rosemead, so we left. Well, in a very real sense, I used to be Groovy Freedom, so I can fully understand what she thought and how she felt once you gave her a checkbook and she realized all the good things she could do with that money. I guess she figured it didn't matter where the money came from, as long as it went to a good cause."

I nodded and sighed. Groovy Freedom's charitable donations were my problem, whether I liked it or not. I would have felt better if she had ripped off Francis Minut Middle School directly and then escaped into the wilderness. At least I could have easily explained it to the school board, and we had insurance for that sort of thing.

The job of principal of Valley High would not go to someone who had made himself look like a fool.

I needed to cancel the dance and balance the Student Activity Fund, even if it meant paying out my own money.

Chris Davis was right. This whole mess was my fault, but she didn't really understand the deeper reason. I had long ago figured out that the kids often elected some unpopular kid as their Grade 8 president as a gag: I knew this but did nothing about it, which was my way of sending them the message that it was OK to do such a thing. In truth, I assumed that their practical joke would come back and bite them on the butt.

I just didn't know it would bite *me* on the butt, too.

24

From the mind of…
ERIN LANGE

I DIDN'T KNOW what to think about any of it. I really didn't.

So Groovy goes out there in a Tigers uniform and gets flattened by the Destroyers. Then Storm goes after Horror Wits and ends up hitting Groovy, and they take her away in an ambulance. That's too sad. I'm never speaking to Storm again, no matter how cute he is.

Where has Groovy gone, anyway?

Well, for the first little while, I guess everyone expected her to be absent from F Minus because of her injuries. Plus, she was a no-show for the Destroyers game on Saturday. It really blew chunks that our Grade 8 president wasn't present at a big event like a football game. Heather showed up, of course, but only because she was our head cheerleader. She said they had the worst turnout ever for a football game. F Minus and Hamber tied at 3, like it actually matters.

I waited and waited for Groovy's return, and soon it became a week since we'd last seen our prez. I missed her extra-much because she had become an extra-special person to me. Also, the Halloween dance was set for Saturday night, and we—or at least

I—really, really, really needed her to be there.

I asked Mrs. Sullings, my homeroom teacher, when we should expect Groovy to return.

"Probably never."

"Whaddya mean? She's our prez! She can't just up and split!"

"I believe she already has."

I crossed my arms and said, "I won't accept that. I'm going to ask Mr. Epperman about this."

"It was Mr. Epperman who told me what I've just told *you*." Then, "Don't go asking him about Groovy. He's already very shaken up about what happened to her."

"But we have a *dance* on Saturday night! Who's going to *run* it?" I felt a little embarrassed about how whiny I sounded.

She looked down at her desktop. "There will be an announcement later on today. We're canceling the dance."

"*No!*" I felt like a little kid again, carrying on because I didn't get my own way. It was not a good feeling, and I probably would have deserved it if Mrs. Sullings had taken me over her knee just then and spanked my butt. Instead, she ordered me out of the room.

In our town, F Minus was the only middle school. It had been around forever, and so had its Halloween dance. So how could they cancel it?

"Epperman is such a doofus," Heather said. "He flies off to Chicago or wherever to hang out at some principals' conference, then he comes back and finds out the students' kitty is empty. So he's, like, 'No money, no dance. Too bad.' I mean, couldn't Epperman get the money from somewhere else? He always seems to find the money for the things *he* thinks are important for F Minus."

"Besides, F Minus is *known* for its Halloween dance," I said. "It's our *thing*, man. That dance is always such a *gas*. And now it's been canceled. How can they do that to us?"

Gabe said, "Epperman isn't the problem here. I can't remember the last time the grownups who think they run this school actually paid much attention to what the students do? That's why the kids around here say, 'The cliques here run this place.' If that's true, it's because the grownups *let* us run it." He added, "It's Groovy's fault that the dance was canceled."

"Excuse me?" I said. "She's not even here."

He nodded. "That's right. It's *her* party, and she isn't even here."

"She isn't here," I told him, "because Beeson punched her out."

"Not my fault that Beeson lost his cool, went after Horror Wits and got Groovy instead."

"When was the last time you actually admitted, 'Yeah, I blew it, it was my fault'? Never, that's when," I said. "When Heather first said, 'Let's pick on Groovy,' you were totally for it. Well, Gabe, I hope you're happy now that you have succeeded in making yourself the biggest jerk in the history of F Minus."

I loved the hurt look on Gabe's face. He was like Storm—those who disliked him also feared him. Therefore, at school, Gabe rarely heard people criticize him the way I had just done. Normally, when treated in any way with disrespect, he would simply shove the kid's head through the nearest wall. But I was a girl, so he couldn't hit me.

"Gee, Gabe," I said, "they said the dance was canceled due to 'regrettable circumstances.' Do you think that maybe that's more than just a dumb excuse? That maybe something tragic has happened to Groovy?"

"I need to check this out," said Heather, who had many ways to do so. She could be one tough chick, and a fearsome adversary, but she also had common sense. Plus, she knew people, and she knew people who knew other people. All of them would be happy to do her a favor now and again. One of those people, Luis, was basically F Minus's office flunky, so she asked him to wait till no one was looking, then pull Groovy's file and show it to us.

"It's *empty*," Heather said, her face contorted in rage and frustration. "Why?"

Luis shrugged. "It's supposed to be full of stuff like emergency contact info plus documents from her old school."

"Exactly," I told them. "We need that. After all, this is a big deal. It's a crisis." Our crisis much more than Groovy's.

"Don't freak out just yet," said Heather. "I'm sure there's someone around here with that information."

I had taken the same school bus as Groovy, but I always got off before she did, so I had no idea of where her residence was.

But by that afternoon, Heather said, "I did some asking around, and guess what? Barb Framer said that her older sister Janine had dated someone named Stef Davis, and that Stef had some hippie chick staying with them." She gave us her big, smug, "Aren't I somethin'?" smile. "Gotta be her, right?"

So she and I boarded Groovy's bus and got off at

the right stop. We walked a block or two and found the place, a fairly big, well-maintained house very much like most of the others in the neighborhood. I felt glad to know that during her time at F Minus, Groovy at least had a nice place to come home to.

"Here we are," Heather said. "Five-eight-zero Dover." She rang the doorbell.

Just then I noticed the car parked in the driveway. I heard its horn honk a bit and its driver's-side winow rolled down. A very good-looking high school boy stuck his head out and said, "Something you need?"

"We're looking for Groovy Freedom," I said.

"Not here," he said. "Gone."

The passenger's door opened and a slim older lady got out. "Groovy has moved out." She spoke the words slowly and with care, as if someone was writing down what she said.

"Do you know where she is?" Heather asked. "We would like to reconnect with her. It would mean a lot to us."

The lady just shook her head.

The boy in the car said, "Sorry we can't help you. I'm getting driver's lessons right now. Gotta go. See ya."

"Not even a phone number?" Heather shot back.

"Where she's gone to," he said, "they don't need phones."

They pulled out and sped off.

As we stood on the porch and watched them disappear, Heather cleared her throat and said, "I hope I'm wrong, but I have a feeling about why we can't find Groovy."

25

From the mind of…
GABE REEDER

EVERYBODY HAD A rumor to spread about what had happened to Groovy. She was in the hospital, or being prepared for an autopsy. She was catatonic… she had lost all feeling from the neck down…she was in the belly of a shark that was swimming in the Pacific Ocean…

I had decided that F Minus was full of imbeciles. I thought they could raise money by holding a raffle. First prize would be Canada.

I had no clue as to where Groovy Freedom was, and, to tell the truth, I was starting not to care. My year of glory was turning into a nightmare, and my name had become a joke at F Minus. I, Gabe Reeder, who had once shared Big Man on Campus honors with Storm Beeson, was now just another big, dumb jock, a guy worthy of no one's respect.

Everyone kept yakking away about Groovy Freedom. Every conversation eventually got around to the subject of our missing prez. The teachers were, like, 'Can we stop talking about her and get on with the day's lesson, please?' At first, I thought the kids were just really disappointed because our Halloween dance had been called off. But then I realized that they were genuinely concerned about her welfare!

"Well, what of it?" I asked. "She was here, now she's gone. Doesn't mean she's dead. Maybe she just went back to Planet Fringus."

Erin shot me her nastiest, dirtiest scowl. "You never liked her! You were always making fun of her!" For a pretty girl, Erin could sure look ugly when she tried to do so. Funny, but I used to think that she was horny for me. Now she just thought I was ridiculous.

"Yeah, I picked on her. So did you. So did most of the kids at this school." Then, "Especially *you*, Heather. You were, like, 'That new girl is so weird and different, let's humiliate her as much as we can.' Of course, you were Heather Marcus, Queen of F Minus, so we did as you said."

"Can you blame me for getting so uptight around her?" Heather retorted. "She held a funeral for a dead snake! She did yoga on the front lawn of the school! She listened to that old-fashioned music—the Great Deadbeats, or whatever you call it."

"The Grateful Dead," I told her. "Their fans call themselves Deadheads."

Erin said, "Groovy gave her life—"

"She ain't dead yet," I replied.

"Maybe she is," said Heather.

Heather always seemed to be the World's Greatest Expert on Practically Everything. If she called CNN and said, "California has just broken away and floated into the ocean," they would probably make it their top story. Groovy had done us many good deeds, and for that we punished her.

"Missing doesn't necessarily mean dead," I pointed out. "I can't tell you where Justin Bieber is at this moment, but I'm pretty sure he's alive and well."

I may as well have been talking to myself. Groovy

136

was here, then she left; none of us knew how to contact her, so she must have given into despair and hanged herself. Right? More accurately, Heather Marcus and her crew had driven the poor girl to suicidal despair. Kids throughout F Minus gave me contemptuous looks as I walked through the hallways.

"It sucks to be me," I told Eugene Horowitz in the cafeteria.

"You mean because of Groovy? You have to admit that it looked bad for you and your clique when she left school in an ambulance. Nobody likes a bully."

"You calling me a bully?"

He stuck out his chest. "What if I am?"

I shrugged. "You're entitled to your opinion. Besides, you're the only one now who will have lunch with me." I thought that if I could hire Dog the Bounty Hunter to find Groovy, once we caught up with her I wouldn't be able to decide whether to take her back to F Minus with me or hide out with her for the next few decades.

"Being a pariah is something I'm used to," Eugene said, "but it's never been something I've liked."

"You've brought on a lot of it yourself," I told him.

"Oh, so when I've been mistreated, I deserved it?" He paused. "You must take a great deal of comfort in that thought."

"From the day we met, you practically had a KICK ME sign on your back. Your hair, your clothes, your glasses—you could have starred in *Revenge of the Nerds*."

He snarled at me. "If that's me, how would you

describe yourself?"

"I was born cool. I'm tall, muscular and good-looking. I've always known how to dress, walk and talk. I know who's cool and who's not. I hang out with the right people and say the right things. Plus, I'm big and tough, so nobody picks on me. Sure, you've probably already forgotten more math and science and computers than I've ever learned, but what of it? Around here, chess and all that stuff means zero." I added, "But then Groovy came along and put up with all kinds of flak but came out of it very popular. I don't understand any of that."

"Then let me explain. Groovy came to us full of light and love. She spread it around. Her light and love just kept growing and spreading. That's what we remember about her—that gift she left us."

I thought about that for a few minutes and let it sink in. "Eugene," I said at last, "I think I know a way we can help Groovy."

"Too late. She's already gone."

"Not too late. Let's go to the library and I'll show you what we can do."

He nodded and gobbled down the rest of his lunch. In the library, I went to the first available computer and used my student number to log on.

"Heather got some of the geeks to help her create a program so she could send mass emails to the entire F Minus student body. But it's *only* for students—teachers can't access it, and I don't think they know it exists."

"With Heather's big mouth, you never know."

We both chuckled. After a few minutes of keyboarding, I read him the message: "Join us for a tribute to Groovy Freedom, our best prez ever.

Saturday, 7 PM, in the parking lot. THIS IS JUST FOR US. NO TEACHERS MUST KNOW."

With much satisfaction, I hit the SEND button. All F Minus students with cell phones, iPods and iPads—in other words, *everyone*—instantly received our message in their in box.

"You like?" I asked Eugene.

He nodded and smiled. "Me likes."

26

From the mind of...
STEF DAVIS

MY ROAD TEST today. I am pumped up because I know I'm going to shred this deal and get that plastic. Once I have that license, it will mark the unofficial end of my childhood. At sixteen, you can't think of yourself as a man till you can drive a car and not have to mess with lame things like public transportation, bumming rides and walking. Better still, you-know-who had packed her gunny sack and gone back to Fringus. Even the girlfriend scene was looking pretty good: Martina Issy had been checking me out, and I found that moderately flattering.

But the main thing on my mind was passing my road test. My dad had called to wish me luck, and he apologized for not being there to provide all the driving lessons he had promised. I had been mad at him for a little while but forgave him after Groovy and my mom had taken over for him and taught me to drive. It didn't matter to me who did the teaching so long as I got taught.

After my dad and I wasted fifteen minutes with the usual blah-blah-blah, my mom called out to me, "Ready to go get that license?"

"Gotta go, Dad. Talk to you later." Click. To my mom, I said, "That was Dad. He was just apologizing for not helping me with the driving."

She nodded and shrugged, the way she probably did all day as a social worker who could provide far less help than her clients required. "He cares a great deal about you, Stef, but sometimes he just spreads himself too thin."

"Yes, he does."

"Now, don't be bitter. This should be a very happy day for you—don't spoil it with anger."

I reentered the DMW lobby and my mother saw me gritting my teeth and clenching my fists.

"Don't worry, Stef. We can practice some more and you can take the road test again."

I waved her off. "Not now, Mom. I have to go get my picture taken for my license."

She frowned. "You *passed?* Then why do you look so disgusted?"

I looked so disgusted because I *was* disgusted—at myself, for the cruelty I had shown Groovy Freedom. My mom had taken her in because the kid had nowhere else to go, and not for one moment had I made Groovy feel the tiniest bit welcome. For her part, she had shown me kindness and friendship, and she had done me a gigantic favor by helping me learn to drive. My mom had done her best to help me with my driving, but Groovy had been my real teacher.

I couldn't very well say, "Mom, I'm mad at myself because Groovy and I sneaked out for driving lessons while you were off doing something else, and she was the one who really taught me. Yes, Mom, I went out

141

driving with a thirteen-year-old girl in *your* car. Hope you're OK with that."

I stepped up, paid my money and affected a tough-guy look as they snapped my picture for my license. I had trouble feeling good about it, though, because I no longer felt I deserved it. Why should this good thing happen to a despicable individual like me?

I wanted to apologize to her, and make it up to her in some way. But I couldn't do that, either. She had gone back to that farm, to pick fruit and listen to folk music with that weird old dude she called Weed. What a shame. What a waste of a life.

Back in Grade 8, I looked forward to growing up and having many, many good times. But Groovy wasn't meant for any of that. She was stuck out there in Rosemead, poor girl.

Tomorrow, Halloween, was the best time of the year to be in middle school. They always threw the best party in town. But Groovy would miss all that. She wouldn't get to party, get loose, boogie with the boys, none of that.

She'd miss it all.

Or would she…?

27

From the mind of…
GROOVY FREEDOM

I CHECKED THE fruits and found them less than perfect. Everything at Rosemead seemed to lack the Tender Loving Care—TLC—that it was used to.

Weed got along on his stick, but his recent medical problems had weakened him, and I didn't know how long he would need to get back to one hundred percent. That meant I had to work twice as hard.

On the positive side, our veggies—potatoes, carrots and turnips—were looking fine and dandy.

Also, Weed *was* getting stronger, and had gotten the best medicine possible—a return to Rosemead. Within a couple of days, he had started driving the truck into town to get supplies. He even insisted that he go alone while I stayed at the farm.

"I can manage all right by myself," he said. "Plus, you have more than enough to do here."

He might have added, "I think you've had your fill of the real world for a while. Getting knock down by the football team, punched by that big bully…? Oh, I think you're better off here, getting the farm ready for winter."

I was home at Rosemead, my own Rosemead, the only real home I had ever had, and I was delighted to be back.

However...

I could scarcely help myself from mentally traveling back to the hectic corridors of F Minus—its slamming lockers and squealing students. I could still hear their cell phones, video games, iPads and iPods.

The place was overpopulated, disrespectful and often terrifying. But it also had its own music, poetry and energy. At times, I missed it so much that I nearly burst into tears.

As the days went by, I looked through Rosemead, telling myself that this was where I ought to be. But the colors and sounds of nature, and my work that changed very little from day to day, now bored me, and I admitted to myself that this solitary life no longer satisfied me.

Now, then: Which life did I want? When I was at F Minus, I yearned for Rosemead. Back on the farm, I wanted so many of the things that the outside world had shown me. I hungered for food slopped onto my plastic tray by crabby old women wearing sweat-stained uniforms. I wanted to sit on someone's sofa and watch endless reruns of *Too Cool for School*. I wanted to stuff my gear into one of those lockers and spin its dial again. I wanted to stare at Stef Davis some more.

I knew that F Minus's Halloween dance would start soon. As Grade 8 president, I had the responsibility of putting it all together, but did nothing, mostly because I didn't know what to do.

But I thought I should attend the dance, anyway.

I had asked Weed for permission to go.

"Negative," he said. "That's ancient history. We're back here on the farm. You have no reason to go there, and I'm not sure you would get the warmest of welcomes if you did show up."

"But you've always taught me—"

He held up his hand to shush me. "You can talk till your face turns blue and it won't make any difference to me. When you left that school in the ambulance, that was forever. You would accomplish exactly zero by going back there even once. You learned nothing of value at that place. Fortunately, I took you away before they corrupted you any more."

Corrupted. That was one of Weed's favorite words. Corrupt, corrupted, corruption. He seemed to think that while he had been recovering in that uptight rehabilitation center, I had spent my days in a place like Columbine High and my nights at Cabrini-Green. Yes, F Minus and the Davis house were very different from Rosemead, but *different* didn't mean *worse*.

Still, I talked on about F Minus and Mrs. Davis's house, and Weed frowned and grimaced and pouted. Maybe he had a point about my having been contaminated by the outside world. I was more assertive towards him now; before, I never would have dared question his judgment on anything.

Also, I would never have done what I was about to do. I found a scrap of paper and wrote a note that I taped to our refrigerator door. The note read: "Weed, don't be mad at me, but I've got to go out there and see those people again. Expect me when you see me. Best, Groovy."

Since Weed had the truck, I had to hoof it. No big deal—I had already walked a zillion miles in my young life. I knew of a gas station a few miles down the way. Once I got there, maybe I could hitch a ride from some friendly stranger. Or maybe I would just walk all the way to F Minus.

I thought about Weed and how badly he would feel when he got my note. I was thinking those thoughts and not paying much attention to where I was going, and that's probably why I ended up wandering along in the middle of the dirt road when a fancy car came my way. Its driver had to slam on the brakes to prevent knocking me into the next area code.

"Whoa!" I called out. "You nearly hit me!"

The driver rolled down the window and yelled, "Why were you walking in the middle of the road?"

I knew that voice right away. I walked up to the driver. "Stef! What are you doing all the way out here? Rosemead is just down the road."

"Why do you *think* I'm out here? I came here looking for you!"

I looked the car up and down. "Looks like someone got his driver's license."

"Yeah, well, I had a pretty good teacher. Anyway, get your butt in here! I've come to collect you and take you to the F Minus Halloween dance."

I got in and he turned the car around. As we went towards town, Stef asked, "How were you going to get to F Minus tonight, anyway?"

"See that gas station we just passed?"

"Yeah."

"I was just going to walk up to someone as they gassed up and asked them for a ride to school."

Stef laughed, but it was a weird kind of laugh— there was no humor in it, and maybe a little anger. "Do you think that's how the world works?"

"What do you mean?"

"Were you going to walk up to some guy and say,

'Hi, I'm Groovy Freedom, and I need a ride to F Minus. I have no money, so would you drive me there for free?'"

I shrugged. "Something like that, I guess."

He gave another weird little laugh. "I'm glad I found you before you had a chance to do something like that."

As we got into town, I saw buildings and street lights and other cars and lots of people—tall ones, short ones, pretty ones, ugly ones. But I felt as if I were looking at my brothers and sisters; I felt, more and more, that I was part of the human family. I loved Rosemead and nature; I loved animals and trees and birds, but I wasn't one of them. I was a person, and I needed to be around other people.

The sky was black now. The city looked dark, dangerous and exciting. I hoped Weed wasn't pacing up and down at Rosemead, worrying about where I had gone and if I was in any trouble.

"The school is dark," I said. "How come?"

"Beats me," replied Stef. "Let's drive around the corner and check things out."

I felt creeped out as we turned and stopped just before reaching F Minus's main driveway. The parking lot was packed with people but no cars. Each person held a flickering candle, making me feel even more freaked out.

Stef swallowed hard and turned to me. "What's all this about?"

"Looks like the Halloween dance I was supposed to plan."

"But they're all standing still and there is no music.

I nodded. "Plus, they were supposed to have it in the gym, so why is everyone out here in the parking lot?"

"Let's get out," Stef said. Then, "Put this on first."

He handed me a rubber Halloween mask.

"Who's this ugly guy?" I asked.

"His name is Richard Nixon. He used to be a president. My mask is no better. I'm going to be a fine man named Marilyn Manson."

We put on our masks, and as we disappeared into the crowd, I did hear music coming from someone's portable player: the Dead's *Blues for Allah*. One of Weed's favorite albums. Mine, too.

"It's supposed to be a Halloween party," I said to Stef, "but nobody's in costume."

But then I noticed that everyone had long hair, beads and tie-dyed clothing. They were all in costume—as *me*, Groovy Freedom!

"Far out!" I shouted.

28

From the mind of…
MRS. DAVIS

NATURALLY, I WAS worried, if only because Stef was a brand-new driver. Besides, he's my only child, so I'm probably overprotective. I sure wish my son had a father figure in his life, but his father shows very little interest in being there. I liked to think that Stef had enough common sense to avoid running around with the wrong crowd, but even good boys sometimes made bad choices.

To get my mind off the fear that Stef had crashed my car and broken his neck, I went into what had been Groovy's bedroom and straightened it out, which took maybe two minutes. When had I ever met a thirteen-year-old girl who as so tidy? Whenever my son changed his clothes, he just threw them every which way and expected me to pick up after him, which of course I did. But Stef isn't dumb, and he impressed me a great, great deal with his ability to learn to drive. His dad took him out a couple of times, and I went out driving with him as often as I could—which, I admit, wasn't terribly often—and each time, I was just amazed at how quickly his driving skills were coming along! As if he'd been getting road lessons on the side that he wasn't telling me about.

I stood in Groovy's old bedroom, thinking about her struggles and dignity, when my phone rang.

"Chris? This is Rob Epperman. Please meet me at school immediately. There seems to be a disturbance of some kind."

"Maybe because you called off the dance. Could be a student protest."

"No, the janitor called me. The kids are all in the parking lot. They're all dressed as hippies and they're holding candles. He says it's a wake or funeral or something for Groovy Freedom."

My heart pounded. My pulse raced. "For Groovy? Last I heard she had gone back to Rosemead. Do you know something I don't?"

"No, but I've got to get over there immediately. Want to meet me there?"

"I don't have a car right now."

"Then I'll come by and pick you up," he said.

Click.

I put down the phone, not knowing what to think of all this.

29

From the mind of…
EUGENE HOROWITZ

I THOUGHT THAT this meeting in the parking lot was a dumb idea, if only because there were so many of us and we each held at least one candle. Our police department had a helicopter that cruised around on a regular basis, on the lookout for suspicious things, and we were that. Once the chopper spotted us, they would radio down and a car would come by to tell us that we were committing a crime known as "unlawful assembly," and if we didn't get lost immediately, we would go to jail.

But that didn't happen.

Heather had said, "Let's go get candles. It'll be dark in the parking lot, so we'll need light. Cigarette lighters would be better, but they're way too expensive." So we went to a discount store and bought the cheapest candles they had. A major hassle, but we got the candles, and everyone—hundreds of us—stood in the dark, in the parking lot, unlawfully assembled, holding a lit candle for someone who was alive and well. What a freaky scene.

Being bad felt pretty good.

Heather. I had spent most of my young life being afraid of her, feeling horny for her, wondering how it would feel to make out with her and envying her very special social position in our little world. For a dozen reasons, she and I were never going to be chummy, but there were a few things I admired about that girl. She was amazing! Heather probably had trouble remembering how to spell her own name, but she was a public relations wizard who could become whoever she needed to be, and in that parking lot that evening, she made herself out to be Groovy's chief mourner. Quite a change from just days ago, when we knew her as Groovy's chief tormentor.

Getting Groovy all dressed up as a Hamber football player was a cruel, vicious, sick prank. I felt dreadful about participating in such nonsense, especially since I, better than anyone else, had been a target of the Heathers and Gabes for so long. My conscience hurt, but so did my ego: I had been expelled from the chess and computer clubs. Mr. Epperman had also suspended me for a week.

As Groovy would say, "Bummer!"

I walked up to Heather, which until recently was something I would never have had the guts to do. "Are we having fun yet?"

"Shut up and let me enjoy my misery," she murmured, smirking.

I shook my head a little. "I don't know about this, Heather. Some of these kids think Groovy is dead, and others think she's in the hospital. The rest are here because they think this is the place to be right now."

She nodded. "Yeah. I think I'm going to say something." Heather climbed onto the bed of the school district's truck and turned off the portable stereo. She picked up the karaoke microphone and turned it on.

"May I have your attention?" she said, her silky voice booming through the parking lot. Considering how many of us had packed into the parking lot, and what a yappy bunch were most of the time, we were a fairly quiet crowd. Those who spoke were practically whispering. In a moment or two, everyone was silent and staring at the beautiful girl with the microphone. I looked up at her, admiring her dimples, gleaming white teeth and violet eyes.

"Everyone, thank you for joining us this evening. if Groovy were here, we know she would be touched and moved by your presence here. Groovy Freedom was our Grade Eight president for only two months, but what a glorious two months they were!" She paused, swallowed, continued. "She isn't with us here any longer, but I think the best way to remember her is just for us to talk about the ways she enrich our lives—"

A couple of clusters of people promptly broke into smaller groups, and one person—Erin Lange— burrowed up to the truck, climbed aboard and snatched the microphone from Heather. I nearly burst out laughing—second-banana Erin treating Queen Heather that way in front of everyone!

"I was mean to Groovy," Erin said, her voice quavering. "I treated her badly because certain people"—she meant Heather—"said it was the right thing to do. But then I started paying more attention to Groovy, and she taught me that there was a better way to be. She showed me that I could become a better Erin, if that's what I wanted." She wiped away and tear. "I didn't even have a chance to tell her that there was no boy named Ronald McDonald who had a crush on her."

Erin gulped for air, tried to say more but couldn't, and handed the microphone to the overweight Grade 7 girl who stood next in line.

"I'm really fat," the girl said. "I used to hate myself because of my weight, but then I met Groovy. She became my first friend. She taught me to believe in myself and told me to get involved in school activities so that my peers could get to know me and accept me for the beauty I possess inside.

I might have gotten up there and put in my two cents about how I was a better person for having known her, but there were already too many kids waiting to do the same thing. Also, I had a huge lump in my throat that would have just gotten bigger the moment I got to the microphone.

The kids got up, spoke, then got back off the truck.

"Groovy's yoga helped me with my anxiety…"

"She made me see that I should stop bullying my baby brother and sister…"

"I babysit once in a while. Now I'm giving some of my salary to charity…"

"Groovy told me about Vietnam and the 'Sixties. Now I'm getting better grades in history."

I shook my ahead, mostly in disbelief. The F Minus kids believed that the best quality a person could have was to be *cool*, and being cool meant never letting on what was bothering you. There were other words for it: Aloof, detached, standoffish, unaffected, indifferent. But it came down to *cool*, and the opposite of cool, *emotional*, was how these kids were behaving tonight.

They were sharing their pain because they had learned from Groovy that it was OK to be human.

Well, I knew the best thing for me to do was take the microphone and eulogize Groovy even though that lump in my throat hadn't gotten any smaller.

So I climbed on board the We Love Groovy truck and looked down at all the faces, all the long hair, all the lit candles and, more important, spotted a couple of adults who were making some effort at not being seen.

I plucked the microphone out of the hands of a girl as she spoke in mid-sentence about what-all Groovy had done for her.

"My name," I said to the zillion flickering lights, "is Eugene Horowitz. I was Groovy's first friend." I felt short of breath, mostly because hundreds of my peers were staring at me and expected me to say great things. So I gave 'em the best I could.

Looking into the sky, I said, fighting back tears, "Groovy, you were the sister I'd never had and the pal I'd always wanted. How am I ever going to get along without you?"

I could hear people starting to cry, and someone yelled out, "Epperman!" Then I heard a very familiar voice call out, "Be strong, Eugene."

I couldn't see who'd said it, but then someone in a spectacularly ugly mask crept up to the truck, pulled off the mask and said, "No more tears, OK? It's me, Groovy. I'm still here."

30

From the mind of…
GABE REEDER

WELL, WASN'T THAT special. If *I* died tomorrow, I wonder who would show up at *my* funeral. I wonder how many people would even notice that I wasn't there anymore. Who would miss me?

Once Groovy pulled off that awful mask, Eugene lost his balance and fell off the truck. People figured out it was the prez, so they nearly killed her with love. They cried with joy and threw themselves upon her. Farther back in the crowd, people discovered that Epperman had crashed our party.

Some of the bigger guys pulled Groovy away from her worshipers and hoisted her up onto the truck. Someone gave her the microphone and she tried to say something. Yeah, good luck with *that*. Hundreds of screaming, shouting, cheering kids made it sound as if Lady Gaga, not Groovy Freedom, stood before us with a live microphone in her hands.

Groovy stepped here and there, trying to get less uncomfortable. Finally she said, "I thought the party would be indoors."

Everyone howled with laughter. Only thing was, she was being very serious.

"I think it's really far out that so many beautiful

people had me in their hearts and minds tonight," she continued. I'm all right. I'm not dead or anything. I had to go back to Rosemead because Weed got out of the rehab center. I belong there, not here."

Groovy paused and seemed to recognize someone in the audience. I looked where she was looking and saw a tall, skinny old man dressed not unlike the countless kids surrounding him—long hair, tie-dyed T-shirt, raggedy jeans. Groovy offered him a big smile and a little wave, and it didn't take me long to figure out that he was the man who had raised her to be the cool kid she was.

"Weed," she said, her voice soft as the microphone bounced it all over the parking lot and beyond, "I'm sorry I came out here after you said I shouldn't. I did it because I really dug what these kids were into, and I wanted to see that dance for myself. But there's another thing. I wanted to say goodbye to all these people, and I want to speak each person's name as I say goodbye."

So she proceeded to say goodbye to the people she knew by name, and if she didn't know the person's name, she asked for it and spoke it in her goodbye.

She went on and on like this, and when it became clear that she was willing to have a personal moment with everyone, they all stayed just for that. A couple of hours later, she finished up.

Groovy tried to climb off the truck, but Storm and I got there in time. We got her onto our shoulders. Erin and Heather joined us as we carried the prez in the direction of the old man Weed.

We had to take our time about it because everyone wanted to give Groovy's hands one last squeeze. When we finally deposited her next to Weed, the old man almost didn't notice because he was getting a ton of attitude from a younger woman.

"Do you *know* what she did with all those checks? It was the school's money, *Weed*, not hers! That was illegal! She could be charged for that!"

Weed frowned. "So you're all bummed out because Groovy gave a bunch of money to charity. Is *that* what you're telling me?"

"You taught her everything she knows," the woman said. "You taught *me* everything I knew till I was twelve. You taught me nothing about the real world. I had to learn that from my parents. They moved out of Rosemead mostly because of you!"

Groovy turned to Weed and said, "I came out here to see the dance. But there was no dance. Are you disappointed in me?"

Weed laughed. "I could *never* be disappointed in you." To the woman, he said, "Later, Christmas."

Everyone said some more loud goodbyes as the two hippies got into a pickup truck and drove off.

The woman Weed had called Christmas hugged a good-looking kid well into his teens. The guy held onto a Halloween mask that was as ugly as Groovy's. Then it hit me: That guy had been Groovy's date! Wow! While Groovy had been making F Minus rethink everything it had ever stood for, she also managed to pick up a boy toy!

The crowd had almost gone away, but there stood Eugene Horowitz, his glasses bent, hair and clothes mussed. He was such a nerd, but now he was also my friend. I couldn't take my friends for granted any longer.

I figured I could learn a lot from that guy.

31

From the mind of…
GROOVY FREEDOM

THERE I WAS, minding my own business, driving our old truck on the road next to our farm when the fuzz busted me again. Weed said I should drive on Rosemead property and I'd be OK, so I didn't get it when the Man put on his lights and pulled me over.

When I said as much to the cop, he said that I wasn't on Rosemead property any longer, that this land now belonged to Marathon Realty. Also, of course, I was still without a driver's license. So he ordered me out of the truck and into the back of his car.

At the little station, the cop didn't handcuff me, he just had me sit there and stare out the window while he got on the phone. I felt my little drive had turned into a bad trip. Weed would be hot when he found out about Marathon Realty. He hated institutions of all kinds, and had started Rosemead so he wouldn't have to mess around with Big Brother or the Man or any of that nonsense any longer.

Weed had kept himself so busy lately, busier than I had ever seen him, and I had a feeling that he wanted to get as much done as he could in the time he had left. He drove to town fairly often, and when he was home he seemed to really enjoy the evenings, when he could sit back and listen to the folk songs he had loved for years. His eyes looked tired and his voice had gotten hoarse. We didn't have those long raps anymore, and I missed them a lot. But he was just too tired for that.

We still didn't have a computer. I was fine with that—Weed and cybernetics wouldn't get along too well.

I'd had a difficult couple of weeks since that Halloween dance that had turned out to be no dance at all. I started to wonder if there was any place in the world for me. F Minus didn't want me, I knew that much. But Rosemead? Well, I guess I had outgrown the farm.

Meeting hundreds upon hundreds of people and seeing them five days a week can be lots of fun. Not seeing those people at all, and being by myself much of the time, can be pretty lame.

I regretted very little about my time at F Minus. I had learned many things, including the fact that when I have a checkbook, I must remember to spend only as much as I have in the account. I learned about lockers and cafeterias and TV.

The main thing I learned was how much more I needed to learn. And now, unlike before, I believed that most of those things were *worth* learning.

I looked through the window and saw a gorgeous, sunlit world full of people and wonderful opportunities. I was missing out on all that, and it made me feel sad and lonely.

Then, a fancy new car glided up into view. Its colorful hood ornament meant it was a BMW, the car they often advertised on the cable channel.

A tall, clean-cut, nattily dressed man got out,

talking on an iPhone. He reached into the car and pulled out a cane.

He had *Weed*'s cane!

The man's hair and clothes were completely different, but he was Weed. *My* Weed. I didn't know what to think.

He came in and gave me a long, heartfelt, Weed-style hug.

"Lookin' good for an old hippie, huh?"

"Weed—what's with the new look? And the car! I don't get it."

He nodded. "Well, Groovy, get ready for some mind-blowing news—"

"I got busted again. The fuzz said that some developer now owns Rosemead."

Weed smiled. "It's true. I sold the property."

"Why would you do that?" I frowned. "You always said—"

"I know what I've always said, and at the time I've always meant it. But times *do* change, Groovy, and we need to change *with* those times."

"I didn't know it was yours to sell," I told him.

"Oh, but it was. When we first started Rosemead back before you were born, I had to borrow some money from my folks to become a part-owner of the land. Over time, families bought in, fell in and out of love with commune life, and I bought them out. For quite a while now I have been the sole owner of Rosemead, and the value has gone crazy. As part of the deal, I made them promise to build affordable housing on the Rosemead site, and a meditation garden for everyone to enjoy."

"But your ideals!" I practically cried out. "Our ideals! We lived there to get away from the power and politics and profits. Now you're saying that you're willing to give that up for money."

"Not at all," Weed said, his voice gentle and quiet, as if he'd expected me to say such things. "Groovy, I sold Rosemead as a special favor to you."

"For real?"

"Yes. After I fell off the ladder and hurt myself, I had all kinds of time to think about things. I'm gonna live for a while yet, I think, but *you're* gonna be here long after *I've* turned to dust. At Rosemead, you and I were just hiding out from the real world. It would have been awful of me to keep hiding out with you till I died, and then you would have had to deal with the real world without me to fall back on and explain things to you.

I felt as if my whole world, even my whole cosmos, had somehow collapsed upon me. Was the man standing before me Weed, or someone else occupying his withered old body? But then I thought for a moment and realized that this was the real Weed. While I had grown up in Rosemead, with the farm being all I had ever known, Weed had spent many years as a youngster in San Francisco, so he knew his way very well in the real world. *I*, not he, was the innocent, backwards hippie kid.

"You know," he said with the mischievous smile I had always loved, "many far-out things have happened to the northern California real estate market since I got ownership of Rosemead back during the Summer of Love. I've just sold Rosemead for twenty million dollars."

"That's a lot of bread, right?"

"That's more bread than you could eat in a hundred years. But being rich doesn't mean selling out. No way! We're not forgetting the ideals that Rosemead represents. With this bread, we can do more good than we ever imagined. You did some good work with those checks you got from F Minus, so I'm thinking we can start the Rosemead Foundation. The spirit of the 'Sixties lives on, Groovy! Far out!"

"But what happens now? To us."

"I've bought us a brand-new condo. They're still building it, but it will be ready soon. I've already got you a place to stay with a family near your new school."

I sighed. "Bummer."

"Oh, I think you'll be happy in this arrangement." Weed pulled out an iPhone and punched a number. He handed it to me.

"Hello?" I said.

"Hey, Little Miss Woodstock." I smiled at the sound of the familiar voice. "I hear you're moving back in with us."

"I think I can guess the name of the new school." I laughed out loud.

Weed laughed, too. "I think there are hundreds and hundreds of students who will be very happy that you're back."

Yeah, and I could remember many of their names.